Y0-GWM-893

MYSTERIES OF ASPEN FALLS™

Breeding Discontent

Johnnie Alexander

Annie's®

AnniesFiction.com

Books in the Aspen Falls Mysteries series

Foal Me Once
Dogged Deception
Tell Tail Clues
The Claus Will Come Out
Worst in Snow
Bones to Pick
Hounded by the Past
Paw & Order
Rapid Decline
Breeding Discontent
Justice Swerved
Away and in Danger

Breeding Discontent
Copyright © 2022 Annie's.

All rights reserved. No part of this publication may be reproduced, stored in a retrieval system, or transmitted in any form or by any means—electronic, mechanical, photocopying, recording or otherwise—without the prior written permission of the publisher. The only exception is brief quotations in printed reviews. For information address Annie's, 306 East Parr Road, Berne, Indiana 46711-1138.

The characters and events in this book are fictional, and any resemblance to actual persons or events is coincidental.

Library of Congress-in-Publication Data
Breeding Discontent / by Johnnie Alexander
p. cm.
I. Title
2022938093

AnniesFiction.com
(800) 282-6643
Mysteries of Aspen Falls™
Series Creator: Shari Lohner
Series Editor: Elizabeth Morrissey
Cover Illustrator: Gregory Copeland

10 11 12 13 14 | Printed in China | 9 8 7 6 5 4 3 2 1

1

Ashley Hart, dressed in khaki shorts and a green tank top, opened the back of her Subaru Outback and pulled out a camp chair. As she set up the chair, she gazed over the spectacular vista before her. Though she'd lived in the quaint mountain village of Aspen Falls, Colorado, for a while, she still often found herself overwhelmed with the grandeur and majesty of the snowcapped peaks surrounding her adopted hometown.

She had parked in a grassy spot off a dirt-packed lane that wound its way through stands of aspen and pine trees, and across lush meadows for several miles from one mountain ridge to another. From her vantage point, she could see where the lane emerged from a stand of thick trees to descend into a pasture dotted with Hereford cattle munching on the abundant grass.

On the other side of the road from the herd, three elk also grazed. The largest sported a giant set of antlers adorned with small, jutting tines. Given time, the young male's crowning glory would become enormous. Ashley had read that the antlers on a mature bull could weigh forty pounds.

The lane meandered through the meadow, then sloped upward through brush and boulders to the plateau where Ashley had parked. She positioned the chair where she'd have the best view of the elk and the lane, grabbed a bottle of lemonade from the cooler she'd brought with her, and collapsed into her seat.

"Moving here was one of the best decisions of my life," she murmured.

A woof of agreement from her Dalmatian, Max, brought a grin to her face. He finished his cursory inspection of the clearing, then flopped down beside Ashley's chair.

With the hot July sun offset by cooling breezes and the murmur of life—soft birdsong, chattering squirrels, and a symphony of insect voices—surrounding her, Ashley released a contented sigh. Her heart felt as if it might burst with gratitude for the blessing of such a tranquil moment. She longed for more relaxing moments, but her busy schedule as the sole veterinarian in and around Aspen Falls didn't allow her many opportunities for such getaways.

That was the main reason she'd jumped at the chance to be a member of the assistance crew for Talons Grip, a team participating in the upcoming Eagle County Adventure Race. While she waited for the three team members to arrive at her designated checkpoint, she could privately indulge in the beauty that surrounded her.

Okay, she admitted to herself, *that might have been the main reason, but my other reason was a close second.* She'd said yes because her boyfriend, Cole Hawke, was the team's captain, and being on the assistance crew meant more opportunities for them to be together. As a U.S. Park Ranger often on call for emergencies in the White River National Forest, Cole's schedule could be every bit as packed as Ashley's.

Thinking of her relationship with Cole reminded her of their first official date, which had memorably taken place on the nearby Weathersby ranch after an emergency call to help a first-time mama deliver her calf. Having interrupted Ashley and Cole's original plans, the cow's owners had served a romantic dinner to the budding couple in their heated gazebo. Ashley would be forever grateful to the Weathersbys—and their cows—for the unforgettable experience.

In fact, the mama and her baby might be part of the Hereford herd grazing in the pasture, though Ashley had no idea how to access the ranch itself from her current location. She'd only managed to find the plateau by following Cole's very explicit and detailed written directions.

Thankfully, Rob Tavish, the team's crew chief, had tied a red bandanna to a stake on the edge of the grassy parking space so Ashley knew she was in the right place. As captain, Cole had adopted the red bandanna to distinguish the Talons Grip team from their primary rivals, the Fighting Fit, who opted for blue bandannas.

Since both teams represented Aspen Falls and two of the opponents—Fighting Fit captain Dina Ford and Rob's wife, Lorie—co-owned Summit Fitness Studio, the competitive spirit was steeped in good-natured ribbing and over-the-top boasting. When it came to the day of the Eagle County Adventure Race, less than three weeks away, Ashley was certain the members of each team would exert all their strength and effort to best the other one—then turn around and cheer for their rivals against all the other competitors.

The young elk buck suddenly raised his head to stare at the spot where the lane emerged from the trees. After a brief pause, he trotted into the safety of the forest, followed by his two companions. Max stood, his nose pointed toward the meadow, and whined. A moment later, a figure pedaled a mountain bike into view, quickly followed by two more. Clouds of dust swirled around the wheels as the three racers made their way across the meadow toward the upward path.

Ashley wasn't surprised when she saw that incredibly fit and well-muscled Josiah Hunter led the team. He and Cole had grown up together, then lost touch when Josiah enlisted in the army after high school graduation. Though he was a decorated soldier and worked as a criminal investigation agent for the military, Josiah had decided to retire after one too many heart-wrenching cases. Besides, he was nearing forty and ready to settle down. He and

Cole had reconnected when he'd moved back to town, and Cole had confided to Ashley that it felt as if he and his old friend were picking up where they'd left off.

Close behind Josiah came the dark-haired, green-eyed athletic ranger who caused Ashley's heart rate to kick up a notch. A graduate of Colorado State University with a bachelor's degree in natural resource management, Cole worked in the Eagle-Holy Cross Ranger District. Few people were as familiar with the mountains as Cole, who loved spending time in them whether for work or play.

Lorie Tavish brought up the rear, but she didn't lag too far behind the men. In her early thirties, Lorie was the youngest member of the team and in great physical shape.

The Eagle County Adventure Race involved hiking, biking, and kayaking along a wilderness course. Rob had set up a practice course that began with a hike into the mountains. He'd been at the first checkpoint, where the hike ended, with the racers' bikes. Ashley was stationed at the midpoint of the practice course with water and energy bars before the team continued biking along the lane to the river. Rob had driven from the first checkpoint to the river and waited there with their kayaks. Once they were on the water, Rob would load up the bikes and drive to the kayaks' end point. The plan was for Ashley to drive to the end point after the racers left her checkpoint.

Several of the cattle in the herd lifted their heads as the racers sped past, then returned to their grazing. Before long, the trio had started their ascent. Ashley rose from her chair and went to the Outback. She raised the hatch, then grabbed a few bottles of water from the cooler and arranged them on the tailgate along with a basket of energy bars and containers of trail mix.

A moment later, Josiah emerged from the brush marking the end of the lane with Cole and Lorie behind him. Josiah braked but remained straddled on his bike while he unstrapped his helmet. "You're a sight for sore eyes," he said with a grin. "I was really hoping for the checkpoint to be at the top of this lane."

"Sorry it's a temporary break." Ashley handed him a water bottle. Her gaze shifted to Cole as he pedaled over the rise and braked to a stop beside her.

"I sure am glad we don't have dance class tonight," he said while removing his helmet. "My legs are too done in for any do-si-doing."

Lorie joined them. "You're taking dance classes?" Disbelief filled her tone as her eyes flicked from Cole to Ashley. "How did you talk him into doing that? I've been begging Rob to sign up with me, but he insists he has two left feet." She accepted the water bottle Ashley handed her as her expression morphed from mock irritation to joking confession. "Admittedly, he does. But still, it sounds like fun. Is it fun?"

Ashley chuckled at Lorie's eagerness. "We've only gone once, and yes, it's fun. We're taking the line dancing class, not square dancing, so we haven't had any do-si-dos yet. You should come. It's on Monday nights at Loggers Saloon."

"That's convenient for you." Josiah tossed a bag of the trail mix to Cole. "All you have to do is walk downstairs."

"Definitely one of the perks of living above the place." The second floor of the old building, an actual Wild West saloon, had been renovated several years ago into four one-bedroom condos, one of which Cole rented. "If a vacancy opens up, you should grab it."

"As much as I'd enjoy having you as a neighbor," Josiah said, "it's past time for me to stake a claim on a place with a little more elbow room. Luke Owens is taking me to a couple of properties this afternoon."

"Luke has been in the realty business for a long time." Lorie rubbed sunscreen onto her arms. "He found the perfect home for Rob and me when we moved here."

"Me too." A mental picture of Ashley's cozy log home in town flashed in her mind, giving her a warm feeling. "Hopefully you'll find your dream house soon."

"The sooner the better," Josiah replied. "During my years in the army, I slept in tents, underneath vehicles, and once in a shipping container. But I'd choose any one of those over many more nights at The Hitching Post. The main thing going for that motel is the price."

Cole downed the rest of his water. "I keep telling you I've got a couch with your name on it."

"You're seriously staying at The Hitching Post?" Lorie's eyes rounded into two china blue saucers. "Does Rob know this? Did he tell you we've got a guest room? Why aren't you staying with us?"

Josiah held up both hands, either to signal Lorie to stop asking so many questions or in surrender—Ashley couldn't decide which. Lorie's exuberance could be overwhelming, but her heart was always in the right place.

"I appreciate the offer," Josiah said. "From both of you. But—"

"I know," Cole said quietly. Ashley gave him a questioning look, and he graced her with a small smile.

"I don't," Lorie declared. "That old motel probably has bedbugs, if not something worse."

Josiah chuckled. "I've dealt with worse, believe me." Still straddling his bike, he pressed his hands against his thighs and shifted his gaze to the path they'd ridden to reach the plateau. Ashley guessed that he saw more than boulders and brush and Hereford cows grazing in the pasture.

"Sometimes even an old fleabag hotel can be a refuge," Cole said.

"Sometimes," Josiah murmured, then gave them a smile. "We're losing minutes. You two ready?"

"Where do we go from here?" Lorie asked.

Ashley pointed to the edge of the plateau where another red bandanna hung from a stake. "That's your entry point, but you have to navigate your way to your kayaks. I've got the coordinates for you." She handed each of them a laminated card that Rob had prepared.

As team captain, Cole pulled up the navigation app on his phone to determine the best route from the plateau to the kayaks. "There are two different paths we could take. At least, it appears there are two that Rob expects us to choose from." His mouth widened into a mischievous grin.

"But?" Lorie prompted.

Cole tapped his screen. "I know a shortcut."

Ashley's heart lurched. Although Cole had roamed these mountains for years, even seasoned hikers and bikers could get lost. "Are you sure?"

"It'll mean carrying our bikes across a couple of rough patches," he said, the confidence in his voice giving her no confidence at all. "But it'll save us a good ten minutes. We can catch Rob napping."

"I love it." Lorie grinned as she adjusted her helmet over her short, white-blonde hair. The stylish pixie cut perfectly framed her petite features. "Let's go."

"One second." Josiah pulled his phone from his sleeve pocket and frowned at the screen. "Sorry. I should take this." He tapped the screen. "Hey, Rylee. I can't talk long."

"Who's Rylee?" Lorie whispered to Ashley.

Ashley shrugged and raised an eyebrow at Cole. "Cousin," he told them.

Lorie's face fell. "That's no fun. I was hoping she was a girlfriend or something."

"Rylee?" Josiah's tone took on a sense of urgency. "Rylee, honey, I can't understand you." He put the call on speaker.

"He's—he's trying to run me..." The voice, young and high-pitched, dissolved into sobs. "Trying to run me off the road!"

"Who is?" Josiah asked. "Where are you?"

"This guy. On a motorcy—" The hysterical voice broke off with a shriek.

"What happened?" Josiah demanded.

"He hit my bumper," the girl managed to eke out between sobs. The sound of an accelerating vehicle came through the phone, followed by a loud report.

A gunshot? It couldn't be. Ashley stared at Josiah, whose face had paled beneath his summer tan. She sidled closer to Cole, and he placed his arm around her shoulder. She leaned into him, wishing there was something she could do—that any of them could do—to help the young woman on the other end of the frightening phone call.

"Rylee?" Despite the fear in his eyes, Josiah's voice remained calm and strong. His military training clearly helped him to maintain control of his emotions. Ashley had a feeling that if his young cousin could see his face, even his eyes would show no sign of fear. "Rylee, please answer me."

"Josey." The sob-wracked voice was barely audible. "He's trying to kill me."

A range of emotions flitted across Josiah's face. "Tell me where you are. I'm coming for you."

The words were barely out of his mouth when Rylee screamed. A sickening crunch immediately followed. Ashley gasped and put a hand over her mouth as Cole's grip on her shoulder tightened. More sounds, muffled and unidentifiable—none of them good—came through the phone.

"Rylee!" Josiah's face blanched as he repeated his cousin's name again and again.

Even after the line went dead.

2

W*e have to find Rylee.* That thought circled in a continuous loop through Ashley's mind even as her feet remained rooted to the ground, unable to tear her eyes away from Josiah's stricken expression as he alternately stared at his phone's screen and hit buttons to reconnect the call. But Rylee wasn't answering.

Ashley became aware of Cole saying something into his phone at her side. "Hey, Angie. A friend of mine was talking to his cousin on the phone when someone tried to run her off the road. There may have been a gunshot."

The fog lifted, and Ashley strode toward Josiah. She laid a comforting hand on his arm. "Cole is talking to Angie Sherman. She's the receptionist at the police department."

Her touch seemed to pull Josiah from his own haze. "I have to find her. She was driving here from Oklahoma City."

"Then she probably took Highway 25," Lorie said, her tone as grave as her expression. The frightening call had smothered her usual exuberance. "It's the most direct route. Was she going to The Hitching Post?"

Josiah shook his head. "We were to meet in town. I made a reservation for her at the Lone Elk."

"Good choice." A slight smile flickered on Lorie's face, and Ashley could guess her thoughts. The ancient motel might be fine for a military veteran, but the Victorian house turned boutique bed-and-breakfast offered much more comfortable lodging for his young cousin.

"Do you know how to get to Highway 25 from here?" Lorie asked.

Ashley had no idea, and it was clear that Josiah wasn't sure either. "Cole must know," she said. "Or I can pull it up on my phone."

"Then you all go ahead," Lorie urged. "I'll call Rob to come get me and the bikes."

Cole joined them. "While I was on the phone with Angie, a 911 call came in about a Dodge van overturned on Alpine Road. We can be there in less than fifteen minutes if Ashley doesn't mind letting me drive."

"I'll stay here with Lorie and wait for Rob." Ashley dug her key fob from her pocket and handed it to him.

"You should go in case she needs medical attention," Lorie insisted. "The ambulance will probably take longer to get there. I'll be fine, and Rob will be here soon. We'll take care of Max and all this stuff." The wave of her hand encompassed the bikes, the cooler, and the camp chair.

Ashley gave her friend a quick hug, told Max to be a good boy, then climbed in the back seat so Josiah could sit in the front with Cole. Frustration hardened Josiah's chiseled features as he tried again and again to reach Rylee. But her phone consistently went to voice mail.

As Cole expertly maneuvered the Outback down the steep mountain track, Ashley was thankful he'd volunteered to drive. Though he took no unnecessary chances, his years of experience driving in extreme terrain allowed him to maintain a higher speed than her comfort would have allowed if she were in the driver's seat.

As the miles slipped by, she mentally reviewed the medical equipment stored in the rear of her vehicle and prayed that she'd be prepared for whatever they found when they arrived at the accident scene.

Once they reached the main road, Cole sped up. He rounded a couple more corners, then slowed to navigate an S curve. As he came out of the curve, he suddenly hit the brakes and swerved.

Ashley braced herself as the Outback came to a sudden stop at an odd angle.

"Did you see that?" Cole cried out. He pointed out the passenger window. "There it is. I almost hit it."

As Ashley stared out her window, movement along the roadside caught her eye. A tan-and-white dog with a collie's double coat and tipped ears limped along the fence row separating the road bank from a field.

"It's injured." Ashley reached for her door, but hesitated as her fingers closed on the handle. Her instinct to comfort and treat the dog—most likely a Shetland sheepdog from its size—needed to be subdued while Rylee's life might be in danger. Every second counted.

"We won't leave it here," Cole said, as if he'd guessed her thoughts. It wouldn't be the first time.

As he carefully straightened the vehicle, another dog appeared beside the road. Even smaller than the first, the newcomer sported long silky ears and a red-and-white coat. As they slowly drove past it, Ashley peered through the glass. "A Cavalier King Charles spaniel," she mused aloud. "I wonder if it belongs to Kristen Marley-Holmes. Her kennel is on the other side of Aspen Falls, though." Surely none of her dogs would be so far from home, or wandering alongside the busy road with a sheltie. She tapped Josiah on the shoulder. "Could they be Rylee's dogs?"

"I wouldn't think so." Josiah's voice sounded strained. "She's the flighty, free-spirit type. Always moving from one place to another, looking for a new lost cause to champion. A pet would tie her down."

"What lost cause brings her to Aspen Falls?" Cole asked, his body tense. He was obviously on full alert as he maneuvered around another bend in the road.

"She's on her way to Wyoming." Josiah released a heavy sigh and ran his fingers along his jawline. "A friend of a friend offered her a job counting antelopes or some such crazy thing. I'll be surprised if she lasts more than a few months."

The moment they rounded the bend, time slowed. A beige van lay on its side in the ditch, perpendicular to the road, with the back hatch flung open. Glass from the front windshield glinted in the bright sunshine. A teenage girl clutching two more dogs, both tiny brown furballs, leaned against the trunk of an older sedan with a dented fender.

Josiah threw open his door before Cole had a chance to put the Outback in park and raced toward the damaged vehicle.

Ashley grabbed her first aid kit and approached the girl. "Are you okay? What happened?"

The teen's eyes welled with unshed tears. "I called 911, but I didn't know what else to do. Someone's still in there." She nodded toward the dogs as she spoke. "These two were on the road. I almost hit them." Her voice broke and she bowed her head.

"Good job rescuing them. Everything is going to be fine. Please stay here." Ashley touched her arm, then hurried toward the van.

Josiah balanced on the corner between the hood and the windshield and reached through the window. "I can't see her because of the airbag. I have to get inside."

Ashley joined him, but she couldn't see inside the vehicle until Josiah moved from his perch, half in and half out of the space.

"Don't cut yourself," she warned. Though the safety glass seemed to have done its job, cracks were visible along the edges of the windshield.

Josiah grunted, then slashed the airbag with his pocketknife. A moment later, he backed out. "She's alive," he said, relief saturating his voice. "I found a pulse."

"That's good," Ashley said. "Don't try to move her."

"I won't." Josiah glanced back at his cousin, then gave Ashley a thin smile. "But that doesn't mean I can't be with her. Make sure she's not bleeding out anywhere."

He gingerly crawled into the vehicle. As soon as he was inside, Ashley positioned herself to peer into the van's interior. The airbag partially hid a young woman whose head slumped against the driver's door, and her chestnut-brown hair obscured her features. The seat belt held her in place, though Ashley doubted she was comfortable.

Josiah balanced above his cousin, using the console and the seat back to brace himself. He gently brushed her hair from her face and checked her pulse again. Bruises covered her forehead, chin, and left cheekbone. She must have hit the door as the van flipped and landed on its side. Blood stained her temple and cheek.

"I think her arm is broken," Josiah said.

Ashley craned her neck, but it was impossible to see past the airbag. She held out the first aid kit to Josiah. "See if anything in there will help."

Cole appeared by her side. "I called Angie again and gave her our exact location," he said. "An ambulance is on the way, and so are Chief Maloney and a couple other officers."

He had barely finished speaking when sirens sounded in the distance, growing louder with each passing second, coming from town—the same direction Cole had driven a few moments earlier.

"The dogs!" Ashley exclaimed.

"Go," Josiah urged. "There's nothing you can do here."

Ashley sprinted around the bend to where she'd last seen the spaniel and the sheltie. When she reached the spot, neither dog was in view. She stopped in the middle of the road, scanning the terrain. The last thing she wanted was for one of the two pups to be hit by a speeding ambulance or police cruiser.

She let out a low whistle, then listened for a response. The wailing sirens made it hard to hear anything else, but she whistled again, then called out in as upbeat a voice as possible. "Here, girl. Here, boy. Let's go."

Once again, she paused and strained to hear. An anguished whimper—surely it wasn't her imagination—caught her attention. She spied both dogs by the fence. Both dogs stared at her. The sheltie lay on the ground while the spaniel stood sideways, ready to run in the opposite direction at the slightest provocation.

Ashley took two slow steps toward them, then crouched down to make herself smaller. "It's okay," she said quietly. "I'm here to help you. To make sure you get home."

The sheltie struggled to stand.

"Did you hurt your leg?" Ashley inched closer.

The spaniel whimpered, unsure whether the stranger could be trusted. The sheltie managed to get to its feet. After emitting a shrill bark, it hobbled toward Ashley on three legs.

Ashley sunk lower and held out one hand. "That's it, sweetheart. Come here. Let me help."

The sheltie's courage seemed to embolden the spaniel, who followed close behind. Ashley sat on the rough ground, legs crisscrossed and shoulders loose. As the two drew closer, she continued talking softly. Suddenly the spaniel ran toward her and sprang into her lap.

"Oh my." Ashley, though stunned by the dog's unexpected rush, held it close. "Aren't you a sweet little thing?"

A moment later, the sheltie dropped in front of her and rested its muzzle on its front paws. Ashley gently scratched its ears, checking beneath the thick coat for a collar. Neither dog had one.

She glanced back down the road, even though the van was out of sight around the bend. "Were you inside that vehicle?" she asked the sheltie, who gazed back at her with intelligent dark eyes as if understanding her every word. The dogs must have been. But why?

The sirens grew louder. Ashley cradled the spaniel under one arm and gently hefted the sheltie as she rose to her feet. When she had them both supported, she stepped farther away from the road. Chief Maloney's familiar department-issue vehicle sped by, followed closely by an ambulance. A second police car also passed her, but braked and then reversed to stop even with Ashley.

The passenger window rolled down, and Officer Wendy Heath peered out at Ashley. "What's going on?"

"I'm not entirely sure," Ashley answered. "The overturned vehicle is around the bend."

"Do you need a hand?" the officer asked as Ashley readjusted her grip on the sheltie.

Ashley gave a grateful smile. "Yes, please. Thanks, Officer Heath."

"How many times do I need to remind you to call me Wendy?" With a grin, the officer reached across the console and opened the passenger door.

"Yes ma'am." Ashley smiled. "I mean Wendy." She used her foot to open the door wider. After sliding inside, she handed the spaniel, the smaller of the two dogs, to Wendy, then nodded toward the sheltie. "This one is injured. I think they were in the accident."

"Did they cause the accident?"

That hadn't occurred to Ashley, but considering what she'd heard of Rylee's earlier conversation with Josiah, it wasn't likely. "Rylee—the van's driver—told her cousin someone was trying to run her off the road. He had the call on speaker, so we all heard it."

Wendy stroked the spaniel, who snuggled as close to her neck and chest as possible. "Who's 'we all?'"

"Cole and me. He's up ahead. And Lorie Tavish heard the call too."

Despite the grim circumstances, Ashley couldn't resist grinning at Wendy. "I think you have a new friend."

"She does seem to like me. Don't you, girl?" The officer handed the spaniel back to Ashley so she could drive. "Maybe she likes me because I'm a redhead like her."

"Could be." Both the spaniel and the sheltie had shiny coats that appeared free of mats. Except for the sheltie's leg injury, they both appeared to be in good health.

Wendy drove forward and parked behind Chief Maloney's vehicle. The EMTs stood beside the van, apparently trying to decide the best way to free Rylee.

"We'd better take the dogs. I'm not sure what department protocol is for canines loose in a cruiser." Wendy unbuckled her seat belt and reached for the spaniel. "I'll take her."

"Thanks. It's hard to hold them both."

As Ashley got out of the car, careful in how she held the injured sheltie, Cole approached. "Glad you got both of them," he said. "Are they okay?"

"This one's scared, but otherwise I think she's okay," Wendy said. "I'd better give her to you, though, so I can help the chief." She reluctantly handed the spaniel to Cole, then headed to the overturned van.

The spaniel stiffened, but slowly relaxed when Cole held her close to his chest. After murmuring a few comforting words to the dog, he asked Ashley, "What about that one?"

"He's injured. I need to look at his leg." The sheltie whimpered and closed his eyes. "Has Rylee regained consciousness?"

"Not yet." Cole tilted his head toward her Subaru. "Ash, I need to show you something."

Ashley glanced toward the teenage girl, who was now sitting sideways in her sedan's driver's seat with her feet on the ground outside the open door and her arms tightly wrapped across her stomach.

"Where are the other two dogs?" Ashley asked Cole as they walked toward the Outback. "Are they hurt?"

"I checked them and didn't see any obvious injuries." Cole nodded toward Rylee's van. "There were two more dogs in one of several crates in the back. The gates on the other crates must have busted open in the crash, because those were the only dogs left in the van. I put them in your car with the other two."

Ashley raised an eyebrow. "Rylee has six dogs?"

"That we know of." Cole scanned the surrounding terrain. "Since there wasn't anything I could do to help Josiah, I wandered around a bit. I didn't find any others, though."

Ashley shook her head in disbelief. What was Josiah's cousin, a young woman who apparently was between jobs and didn't have a home, doing with that many dogs? And not just any dogs, but at least two that were extremely well-groomed purebreds?

Though she hadn't paid too much attention to the two the teenager had saved, Ashley's impression was that they appeared to be some kind of terrier. "I need to see the two the teen was holding."

Cole opened the back of the Subaru. Two small dogs with smooshed-in faces, bearded chins, and short beige coats nestled on a blanket inside a crate. Nearby was a tote with emergency medical supplies.

"They're like a pug mixed with a schnauzer," Cole remarked. "I've never seen dogs like them before. Have you?"

"A couple times," Ashley replied. "They're Brussels griffons." A breed that, in her experience, was less known and even scarcer than a Cavalier King Charles spaniel. Except for the dirt from the road coating their fur, they too appeared well-fed and healthy.

"There's another one like them in a crate I put in the back seat." Cole placed the spaniel with the griffons and latched the crate door again. Then he rounded the rear of the Outback and opened the passenger door. "I think the other one is some kind of chihuahua."

Still holding the sheltie, Ashley followed him and peered into the crate. The barrel-chested griffon whined and pawed at the crate, apparently eager to get out. The other dog cowered in the crate's far corner. Its long coat, with a texture more like hair than fur, was white with black splotches, while its face was mostly black with tan markings around the dark, frightened eyes. The most distinctive feature was its oversized ears.

"He's a papillon, not a chihuahua." Ashley placed her free hand against the metal of the crate so the dogs could sniff her fingers. "*Papillon* is French for 'butterfly.'"

"The ears," Cole said, making the connection. "They do remind me of butterflies. Big black ones."

Another scarce and expensive breed.

Ashley shifted her attention to the crashed van. A gurney stood in a flat space near the front bumper. On the way to the crash site, Josiah had told Ashley and Cole that Rylee was in her early twenties. Their moms were sisters who'd been born almost a decade apart. Josiah's mom was barely out of her teens when he was born while his aunt was in her mid to late twenties when she'd had Rylee. The families lived in different states and weren't close. An occasional Thanksgiving or a summer weekend were about the only times they had spent together.

When he'd gone into the military, though, Rylee had become his pen pal. Her parents had been going through an ugly divorce, and she seemed to need a father figure in her life. After she graduated high school, her care packages, emails, and texts became less frequent. He'd been pleasantly surprised when she'd recently contacted him to see if they could get together.

Josiah hadn't mentioned anything about dogs. Considering he'd made a reservation for Rylee at the Lone Elk Bed-and-Breakfast, he must not have known she was traveling with them. Though Ashley knew the B&B was pet friendly, she doubted owners Liv and Brett Stratton would accommodate six pets for one guest—especially without advance notice.

"Do you think Rylee planned to leave the dogs with someone while she was in Aspen Falls?" Ashley asked.

"Who?"

"I don't know." Ashley lifted the sheltie so she could rest her chin on his soft fur. "Just thinking out loud, I guess."

"Careful there," someone shouted, drawing their attention to the van.

"They're getting her out." Cole jogged toward the vehicle, and Ashley hurried after him.

As she cradled the sheltie, guilt gnawed at her stomach. She should be at her own vehicle tending to the injured dog instead of being a nosy bystander, but her concern for Rylee won out.

From her vantage point off to the side, she watched spellbound as a stretcher emerged from the glassless windshield. Josiah and Chief Maloney helped to guide it through the hole, and Cole stood ready to help.

Rylee, lying beneath a tan blanket, was strapped to the stretcher. A brace surrounded her head and neck, keeping her immobile. An IV bag rested on her chest, and a nasal cannula had been inserted into her nose. Once the stretcher was clear of the vehicle, Wendy steered the gurney closer to the edge of the road.

Ashley couldn't begin to imagine how the EMTs had managed to get the young girl from her seat and onto the stretcher. She rounded the vehicle to join Cole, who stood on the opposite side of the gurney from Josiah. An EMT flashed a light into each of Rylee's eyes, then checked the straps.

Josiah grasped one of his cousin's hands in both of his. Worry hardened his jaw and deepened the furrows around his eyes. Suddenly Rylee's shoulders twitched, and her eyes flew open. Fear clouded her features as she tried unsuccessfully to move her head.

"Shh," Josiah soothed, moving into her sight line. "I'm here and you're going to be okay. Lie still."

Huge tears welled in her eyes and slid down her cheeks. A moan escaped her cut lips. "I didn't mean for this to happen." The words came out cracked and low as she struggled to breathe. "It's all . . . my fault."

3

After Josiah left with Chief Maloney to follow the ambulance, Ashley placed a splint on the sheltie's injured leg while Cole moved the crate to the back seat of the Subaru and placed all the small dogs inside. They were a little crowded, but Ashley preferred them to be in the crate than loose in the vehicle. The slightly larger spaniel sprawled patiently on the floor of the back seat.

"I'm glad Lorie took Max," she said. "One less dog to worry about."

"I'll send her a text to tell her what's happened." Cole pulled out his phone and tapped the screen.

"Could you please ask her to drop Max off at the clinic whenever it's convenient for her?" Ashley glanced at her watch, surprised to find that it wasn't even noon. The morning hours, in a strange way, had seemed to both drag and rush by. The clinic wouldn't open until two, which meant she'd have time to evaluate each of the dogs before any patients arrived.

Wendy appeared with a handful of nylon leashes, each with a metal ring attached to one end that made it possible to fashion a slip collar. Ashley kept similar leashes, emblazoned with the clinic's name and logo, on hand at Happy Tails, but the ones Wendy had found were blank.

"I searched as much of the van as I safely could," Wendy said. "There was a jug of water and a plastic bowl, but no dog food. No collars. No vet records. Nothing."

"Thanks, Wendy. Just put them there." Ashley, who was using the back hatch as a work space, gestured toward a small tote that held collars, leashes, a container of treats, and a few other supplies that she kept in her car for the rare times when she came across a stray dog running loose or injured.

"What do you know about the driver?" Wendy asked.

"She's Josiah Hunter's cousin." Ashley considered what else to say. She didn't want to keep any important information from Wendy, but she didn't want to gossip either. She decided to skip the personal family dynamics, but told the officer that Rylee had come to Aspen Falls to see Josiah while on her way north.

"Did Josiah know she had all these dogs with her?" Wendy asked.

"I don't think so." Ashley placed a strip of green wrap tape around the sterile gauze that held the splints to the sheltie's leg. As soon as she got back to the clinic, she planned to x-ray the limb. Hopefully she wouldn't find a broken bone.

Wendy stroked the sheltie's head. "These are all beautiful dogs. I'm guessing expensive too."

"Most likely."

"Then why aren't they wearing collars? Why is there absolutely no information about them anywhere in that vehicle?" Wendy's green eyes flashed, and her tone grew more animated. "There isn't even food. Who travels with six dogs and no food? Something is off here. I feel it in my bones."

"I agree." There were few dogs in rural Aspen Falls that didn't wear a collar of some type. And Rylee's passengers weren't farm dogs. As snobbish as it might sound, Ashley had a hard time imagining anyone with a King Charles Cavalier spaniel, Brussels griffon, or papillon who wouldn't have a collar on the dog with an ID tag attached.

Wendy released a sigh and lowered her voice. "Is it possible they're stolen?"

The idea had flitted at the edges of Ashley's mind, but she'd repeatedly pushed it away. She didn't know Josiah well, but Cole did.

After all, they'd grown up together. The thought that his cousin could be involved in such a theft wasn't one she wanted to entertain. But Wendy had said the words out loud, and Ashley couldn't hide from them any longer.

"I'll check them for microchips when I get back to the clinic," Ashley said. "Hopefully that will tell us more about them." *And put an end to my suspicions.*

"That's a good idea." Wendy seemed calmer now. "I'm going to take our 911 caller's statement while we wait for the tow truck to arrive. But please let me know if you need volunteers to help care for these little guys. Rich and I can foster the spaniel."

"Are you sure?" Despite being in his early forties, Rich had suffered a heart attack recently. As far as Ashley knew, he still hadn't returned to work.

"I think she's exactly what Rich needs right now," Wendy said. "A little dog to keep him company for a day or two. Besides, Andie has been begging for a dog. This would be a good test run to see if my teenage daughter is as responsible as she thinks she is."

"Every girl should have a dog," Ashley said. "I haven't even thought about what to do with all of them." She'd been too focused on the dogs' immediate health, but they needed to go somewhere. Josiah couldn't take care of them, not as long as he was staying at a motel. And even though she had enough space at the clinic, appropriate foster arrangements would be less stressful for the pups. Though frightened from their ordeal, each of the dogs had responded well to being handled by strangers.

"We'd be happy to help out," Wendy said. "Whatever you need."

"Thanks," Ashley replied. "I'll let you know as soon as we find out more about them."

A sharp series of barks interrupted their conversation. A moment later, a boxer bounded toward them from behind the van.

"What in the world?" Cole said as the boxer raced toward him. The dog slid into a sit, bumping into Cole's shins and nearly knocking him over, then tilted his head and stretched his lips into a goofy smile. "We've got another one," Cole announced as he knelt to rub the dog's ears. "And again, no collar."

Ashley exchanged a glance with Wendy and sighed. "Put him in the back seat," she instructed. "We've got quite a clown car situation happening here."

The boxer bounced into the back seat, sniffed the spaniel and the crate holding the smaller dogs, then curled up into his allotted space.

When Wendy left to talk to the teen, Ashley asked Cole to drive her Outback into town so she could hold the sheltie on her lap. He'd be safer in a crate, but they only had the one taken from Rylee's van. With the smaller dogs crowded inside, there wasn't room for the injured sheltie.

Lorie had offered to let Max hang out with her and Rob for a while, and Ashley was grateful her Dalmatian was in good hands so she could focus on the mystery dogs. On the way to the renovated fire station that housed the veterinary clinic, a law office, a coffee shop, and other businesses, Ashley called Ben Sato, her part-time veterinary assistant. She told him the basics, that a friend's cousin who was traveling with six—no, make that seven—dogs had been in an automobile accident. He agreed to go to the clinic to prepare for Ashley's arrival.

Next she called Holly Kipp, her best friend and the owner of 3 Alarm Fur, a pet grooming service that was also located in the historic fire station. Holly quickly offered to call Fluffy Friends Adoption and Rescue to inquire about temporary foster care for the dogs.

Both Ben and Holly were waiting when Ashley and Cole arrived at the fire station. Soon they settled all the dogs except for the sheltie in separate kennels. Holly took the initiative to create an intake form for each dog even though all she could record was the breed, color, and gender. As Ashley and Ben prepared to x-ray the sheltie's leg, Cole volunteered to jog over to Icebreakers Pub for a take-out order of sandwiches and salads.

After the X-ray was taken, Ashley and Ben peered at the monitor. "I don't see a break," Ben said. "Do you?"

Ashley sighed with relief. "Thankfully, no. Let's give him a full exam in room four and check for a microchip." She gently lifted the dog from the X-ray table.

"I'll get the scanner," Ben said.

Holly clutched a clipboard with the intake forms as she joined them in the examination room. She ran her fingers through the dog's soft coat and behind his ears. "He's been bathed recently. No mats. Even his toenails look freshly clipped."

"He's healthy too. Except for his leg." Ashley shared the vital information—weight, temperature, heart rate, the condition of his gums and teeth—for Holly to record on the form. "Now let's find out if he's chipped."

Ben handed her the scanner, which she poised over the dog's shoulder. At the beep, she read the registry number for Holly to record on the form. When they were finished, Ben took the sheltie to his own kennel and returned with the three griffons. As Ashley examined one, the other two explored the room and enjoyed the treats Ben offered them. The two older females appeared to have given birth before, but not the younger female. To Ashley's relief, all three had microchips.

Cole returned with bags of food and drinks while Ashley was examining the papillon and the spaniel. "Sorry that took so long," he said, his athletic frame filling the doorway. He'd changed from biking gear into a T-shirt and cargo shorts. "I got back to the pub from changing clothes before the order was ready, but it was as if everyone in there wanted to know what happened. News of the accident is all over town."

"Have you heard from Josiah?" Ashley asked.

"I texted him, but he hasn't answered." With his hands full, Cole jutted his chin toward the examining table. "How are the dogs?"

"So far nothing worse than a couple minor scratches," Ashley said. "But the papillon's back is tender so he'll need an X-ray too."

"I don't suppose you'll stop to eat first." Cole's tone made it clear he already knew her answer.

"X-rays first, then food," she said. "The boxer is the last one I need to examine, and there doesn't seem to be anything wrong with him. It won't take long to get his info."

"I can take the X-ray while you examine the boxer," Ben volunteered. "The aroma of that Philly cheesesteak is calling my name."

"Agreed," Ashley said. "I'll be there in a few minutes to go over the X-ray results."

"I'll set up the food in the break room," Cole offered, then grinned. "But don't take too long or there might not be anything left."

A chorus of good-natured protests followed him from the room, and Cole responded with a teasing laugh as he disappeared down the hallway. As Ben left with the papillon, Ashley picked up the spaniel and held her close.

"Wendy Heath volunteered to foster this one," she told Holly. "She thought Rich would enjoy having her while he's recovering."

"That sounds like a great idea to me." Holly set the clipboard on the counter. "She's a sweetie. Actually, they all are. Well-behaved. Well-trained. Well-groomed. Well-everything."

"And yet . . ." Ashley hesitated.

Holly tilted her head. "Yet what?"

"Josiah told Cole and me that his cousin was flighty. His word, not mine." Ashley stroked the spaniel's silky ear. "I'm having a hard time reconciling that the person he described could take such good care of so many dogs."

"Maybe she had them all professionally groomed before starting on her trip," Holly suggested. "I'd say that even the griffons have been recently plucked. That's a time-consuming task."

"It sure is," Ashley agreed. Like many wiry-haired breeds, the griffons' grooming regimen required plucking instead of trimming.

"I don't understand why the smaller dogs, whose coats require special care, look great, but the boxer doesn't." Holly had put him in a kennel, so she'd had an opportunity to check him over. "He's clean, but I doubt he's had a recent bath. Plus, his nails need a trim and his ears could use a good flush. With his short coat, he'd be the simplest one to bathe."

"You're right." Ashley didn't understand the differences in how the dogs had been groomed either. So much about the situation didn't make any sense. "There was no food or personal effects like collars and leashes in the van. Only a gallon jug of water."

Holly's eyes widened. "Where was she driving from?"

"She started out from Oklahoma City."

"With no dog food?"

"I'm not sure. All I know is that there isn't any food now. Or food bowls or collars or vet records. Rylee doesn't have any of the items I make sure I have when I take a road trip with Max. It's as if . . ." She couldn't finish the thought, but she didn't have to. She could tell from the expression on Holly's face that her friend understood what she couldn't say. And that Holly couldn't bring herself to say the words either.

"Go on and get the boxer." Holly grabbed a bottle of cleaner. "I'll sanitize the table for you."

"Thanks." Ashley headed for the kennel room. Each of the dogs seemed to be resting comfortably after their traumatic experience. None of them barked or whined or pawed at the door. Another item to add to the growing list of positives—they were apparently crate trained, each and every single one of them.

Stopping her thoughts from heading down the rabbit trail she wanted to avoid as long as possible, Ashley situated the spaniel in a kennel that Ben had prepared with a soft blanket and a stuffed toy. The spaniel sniffed the blanket, turned around once, then laid down with her head resting on the toy as if it were a pillow.

Ashley bent to open the larger crate holding the boxer. He stood, stretched, then exited the crate with a clownish expression on his face and a bounce to his step. As she looped a slip leash over his head, he nudged her hand with his flattened nose, practically pushing it up to the fur-covered dome between his ears. Ashley obliged by scratching the spot, and he responded by pressing his solid body against her leg.

"Come on, you handsome fella," she said. "Let's make sure you're none the worse for wear from flying around the inside of that van."

The examination didn't take long, and Ashley was pleased to discover that the boxer also had a microchip. She read the number to Holly, who recorded it on the intake form.

Ben entered the room with the papillon, a vial of medicine, and a syringe. "X-rays are fine. It's probably just a bruise. I thought you might want to give him a painkiller, though."

"Thanks, Ben. Put him on the table and I'll give him the shot, then he'll likely be fine." Ashley administered the medicine while Ben kept a firm but gentle hold on the dog and spoke softly to him.

Holly flipped through the pages on her clipboard, then added the painkiller's dosage to the papillon's form.

"I'll take these two back to their kennels." Ben started to leave but Ashley stopped him.

"The boxer can come to the break room with us," she said. "He's such a good boy, and I think he'd like the company."

Ben chuckled. "Showing favoritism to the big breeds again?"

"Doesn't she always?" Holly added with a wide grin.

Ashley's cheeks warmed, mostly because she couldn't deny the kernel of truth in her friends' teasing accusation. She respected and cared about all her patients, but her heart was especially drawn to the working breeds such as her own beloved Dalmatian and the goofy boxer. But she wouldn't admit to either Ben or Holly that they were right. Instead, she glanced at the clock. Already past one. Where had the time gone?

Silly question. She'd examined seven dogs, so of course the time had flown by.

Holly elbowed Ashley and took the clipboard from her. "I don't know about you, but I'm starving. We've left Cole alone with the food too long."

"I should look up those microchip numbers first." Ashley reached for the clipboard, but Holly hid it behind her back.

"Ellen will be here soon, won't she?" Ellen Hayes, the clinic's receptionist and office manager, usually arrived half an hour or so before the clinic opened. "She can do that when she arrives." Holly pointed toward the door. "Eat. Now."

Ashley raised her hands in surrender. "Okay, I'm going." She slipped the leash over the boxer's head again. "Come on, Buster. How would you like a bite of a roast beef wrap?"

In the break room, Cole had set out the sandwiches and drinks on the counter. Ashley didn't realize how hungry she was until she took her first bite of the wrap. The seasoned roast beef slices were tender, and horseradish aioli added another layer of flavor.

The boxer laid at her feet and rested his head on his large paws. A moment later, he rolled onto his back and waved his feet in the air as if he didn't have a care in the world. For the first time, Ashley noticed dark spots on the bottom of his pads. She set her sandwich on a paper plate and bent down beside the dog.

"What's the matter?" Cole asked around a bite of his meatball sub.

"He stepped in something. Maybe mud." Ashley scraped at one of the spots with her fingertip. Dread jolted along her spine.

"I didn't see any mud at the accident scene," Cole said.

"It's not mud." Ashley examined her finger then bent forward and sniffed the boxer's paw. The metallic tang of copper filled her nostrils. "I think it's blood."

4

Ashley got up from her chair and crouched beside the dog. "Stand up, boy," she encouraged him. He took his sweet time doing so until Cole tempted him with a small chunk of meatball. After he stood to take the treat, Ashley ran her fingers once more along his legs, tail, and stomach but didn't find any injuries. "The blood doesn't appear to be his."

"Could it be from one of the other dogs?" Cole asked.

"I don't think so," Holly said. "We gave each of them a thorough going-over. None of them were bleeding."

"Let's take a sample of whatever it is," Ben suggested. He left the break room and soon returned with a damp cotton swab and a plastic bag. While Ashley held the boxer's paw, Ben ran the cotton swab over the dirty pad and placed it in the bag.

When he finished, Ashley grabbed the clipboard from the counter where Holly had placed it. "I can't wait any longer to find out who these dogs belong to. Especially him."

The others followed her to the doctor's station in the large prep area.

Ashley booted up the computer, then opened their client database. "First, let's make sure that we don't already have a file on him." She searched the database for *boxer* and found two. Neither was the boxer currently leaning against Cole's leg. One was a female, the other a six-month-old male. She recognized the names of both families.

Ashley exited the clinic files and brought up a universal microchip registry database where she could narrow down which microchip companies had been used for the dogs.

As Holly read off the boxer's microchip number, Ashley entered it in the search bar. The names of two registries appeared. She copied the microchip number she'd entered and clicked on the more popular of the two registries. After logging in with her clinic's name and password, she pasted the number into the appropriate box. A moment later, the boxer's page, including his photo, appeared on the screen.

"Notice the white blaze on his chest. It's definitely him," Ashley said. "His name is Cliffy."

At the sound of his name, the boxer trotted toward her, and she patted his head.

Cole peered over her shoulder. "I didn't know Oscar Moore had a dog."

"You know him?" Ashley asked in surprise.

"Well enough to say hi when our paths cross." Cole pointed to the address. "He's a local."

"But that doesn't make sense," Ashley said. "What was his dog doing in Rylee's van?"

"Maybe the boxer wasn't in the van," Cole reasoned. "At least not when it wrecked. He could have been roaming the countryside and gotten curious, especially with the other dogs milling around."

"I'll call the number that's listed." Holly pulled out her phone and dialed, then hit the speaker button for all to hear.

"Hello?" an upbeat, elderly voice answered on the fourth ring.

"May I speak to Oscar Moore?" Holly asked.

"No one here by that name. Sorry."

"Please don't hang up," Holly said quickly. "This is the number Mr. Moore left on a pet registry for his dog. A boxer named Cliffy."

"I've had this number a couple of years now," the man said. "Personally, I don't see much need for a landline anymore, but the missus insisted we have one. Gives her comfort, and that's always been my life's goal. The key to a happy marriage, if you ask me, is to give each other as much comfort as possible—and we'll have been married sixty-five happy years and only one miserable one in a couple of weeks."

Holly's dark-brown eyes twinkled. "I hope that miserable one was a long time ago."

"You bet it was. So long ago we almost forgot about it once or twice."

"He's adorable," Holly mouthed to Ashley before returning her attention to the phone call. "Congratulations on your anniversary. I'm sorry to have bothered you."

"No bother at all. I wish I could have been of help, but we don't know anyone by the name of Moore, or anything about a boxer."

Holly ended the call. "Mr. Moore must have canceled his landline service and never updated the registry information."

"I can take Cliffy back to his house," Cole volunteered. "It's a bit of a drive, but I don't mind."

"I'd like to go with you." Ashley had a strange feeling that something involving the boxer was out of sync. She couldn't explain the sensation, but she'd learned to trust her instincts. Even though she couldn't keep Mr. Moore from taking possession of his dog, she wanted to meet him and to assess the home situation. To find out if Cliffy often wandered from home, and what steps Mr. Moore planned to take to keep him from doing so in the future.

"It's odd that Cliffy isn't one of our clients," Ben said, and Ashley immediately realized that Ben had put in words one of the reasons for her uneasiness. "We've been open more than a year. In that time, we've seen practically every dog in the area. I don't know many people who still make the trip to Beaver Creek or Vail."

Before Ashley had moved to Aspen Falls, residents had traveled to veterinarians in Beaver Creek or Vail, both of which were about twenty-five miles away. Though not every cat owner in town brought in their pets, almost all the dog owners did.

"I suppose he could be one of them," she replied. "I'll be sure to ask Mr. Moore if Cliffy is up-to-date on his vaccinations." She printed out the listing page from the registry site to add to the boxer's file, then turned to Ben. "We should take Cliffy home as soon as possible. Who's our first appointment?"

"Hector Slade is bringing in his cat, Tulip, for a blood draw at two," Ben answered. "We scheduled a staff meeting from two thirty until three. At quarter after three, Ruby Wilkins is bringing in the Three Musketeers. We blocked off forty-five minutes for them."

"That will definitely add some excitement to the day," Holly said. The trio of English sheepdogs were wonderful, though they had an almost uncanny knack for finding muddy ditches to play in. On those occasions, when Holly had to bathe, dry, brush, and comb all three of the long-haired and energetic dogs in the same day, she always had stories to tell. "If you need a hand, let me know."

"Thanks," Ashley said absentmindedly. She glanced at the clock, did a quick calculation, and made a decision. "Ben, you can handle the blood draw for Tulip. We can reschedule the staff meeting if necessary. That way, I can go with Cole to take Cliffy home. We'll be back by three, right?"

Cole nodded. "I doubt we'll be gone much more than an hour."

"Okay," Ashley said. "It's a plan."

"I'll go prep for Tulip." Ben disappeared down the hall and into an exam room.

"Want me to check the registries for the other dogs while you're gone?" Holly asked.

"It won't take me very long," Ashley replied, returning to the universal database. "I want to know if any of them belong to Rylee before I leave. Will you read the numbers for me? The sheltie first."

Holly recited the number, and Ashley traced it to the correct registry. As Ashley scanned the information—the dog's registered name was long and pretentious, but his call name was Ashes—Holly gasped.

"His owner lives in Amarillo, Texas," Holly said. "And his name isn't Rylee."

"Strange." Ashley printed the page for the sheltie's file. "Let's do the papillon next." She wanted to contact the owners of the injured dogs before providing more treatment in case they had any allergies she should know about.

The papillon's name was Rugby and his owner, who wasn't Rylee, also lived in Amarillo. A different Amarillo resident owned Bridey, the King Charles Cavalier spaniel.

The three Brussels griffons—Twiggy, Willow, and Maple—all belonged to the same owner, someone with a Canyon, Texas, address. A check on an Internet map showed that the small city was located less than half an hour south of Amarillo.

"Are you thinking what I'm thinking?" Holly asked as she pulled the final three record sheets from the printer and filed them with the corresponding patient intake forms.

Ashley exchanged a long look with her friend. "Yes."

Cole raised an eyebrow. "What am I missing?"

Holly waved the clipboard. "These aren't just purebred dogs. They're show dogs. That's why they're so freshly groomed and perfectly behaved."

"Perhaps Rylee was taking them to a show," Ashley suggested. She still didn't want to think the worst of Josiah's young cousin, but the evidence made it difficult. Her innate honesty made her add, "Except then she'd have their records."

"Is it possible the files are still in the van?" Holly asked. "Maybe hidden beneath a seat?"

"No," Cole said. "I don't know why Rylee had these dogs, but she wasn't taking them to a show. She'd have told Josiah if that's what she was doing. And it doesn't explain why Cliffy was with her. Unless he's a show dog too."

"He could be," Holly said. "Or he might have been at one time. He's a handsome boxer. Granted, he doesn't have a registered name listed on his microchip registry sheet."

"We need to talk to Oscar," Ashley said.

"I'm ready to go when you are," Cole replied.

Ben and Ellen appeared in the prep area. "I hear you've had quite a morning," Ellen said. "Where are all these dogs who're visiting us?"

"In the kennel room," Ashley said, then glanced down. "Except for this beauty. Meet Cliffy."

Ellen immediately knelt in front of the boxer and placed her hands on both sides of his rounded cheeks. He responded by wagging his entire back section, which sent his docked tail waving. "Aren't you a handsome boy?" Ellen cooed. "Yes, you are."

"He belongs to someone named Oscar Moore," Ashley said. "Do you know him?"

"He lives several miles south of town," Cole added.

Ellen tilted her head in thought. Between leaving her job as a school nurse and accepting her position at the clinic, she'd worked a variety of part-time jobs in town, which meant she knew almost everyone. But she seemed to be stumped. "I can't place him," she finally admitted. "It's strange that he hasn't brought Cliffy in for vaccinations, though. Did you check the files?"

"He's not in our client database. Holly filled out sheets on all the dogs, though." Ashley handed the clipboard to Ellen. "Would you please make copies of Cliffy's info? I want to take it with us."

"I'd be glad to." Ellen led the way to the reception area, and the others followed her. First, she checked the file drawers in case the boxer's information had somehow missed being added to the computer database, but she didn't find anything under Oscar Moore's name. Then she made the requested copies and placed them in a manila folder for Ashley.

"Thanks, Ellen." Ashley slipped the leash over Cliffy's head. "We'll be on our way. Ben is handling Hector Slade's appointment, and I'll be back before the Three Musketeers arrive."

"They're the main reason I'm here today," Ellen said. "Thought you might need the extra help."

"I appreciate it." Ashley chuckled. "While we're gone, would you mind calling the other owners and let them know we have their dogs? Call the sheltie and papillon owners first and ask about allergies."

"Will they already know about the accident?" Ellen asked.

Ashley looked to Cole to answer. "I don't see how they could," he said. "Maybe we should check with Chief Maloney before making those calls."

"I'll contact him," Ellen said. "You two go along so you can be back in plenty of time for that unruly trio."

"Call me if you need me." As Ashley guided Cliffy out the door, she wondered what they'd find at the boxer's home. Her mind flashed back to the blood on Cliffy's paws, and she bit back a wave of anxiety about what might await them.

5

Once again, Ashley asked Cole to drive her Outback. He knew the way to Oscar Moore's rural home, and she wanted to keep an eye on Cliffy. Not that she needed to worry about him. The boxer sprawled on the back seat and was snoring loudly before they'd reached the outskirts of town. When they were almost to their destination, Ashley's phone rang.

"Hey, Ellen," Ashley said after connecting the call through the car's hands-free system. "You're on speaker."

"That's fine," Ellen said. "Wendy Heath is here with me. She came to the clinic to check on Bridey right after you left."

Ashley shared a bemused glance with Cole. The police officer was obviously smitten with the spaniel.

"Wendy talked to Chief Maloney and he asked her to make the calls," Ellen continued. "The owners were stunned to hear about the accident, especially since they had no idea their dogs were still in Colorado."

"Where did they expect them to be?" Cole asked.

"On their way home from a four-day dog show in Colorado Springs," Ellen replied. "The owners all belong to the same dog club in Amarillo, and they use the same group of professional handlers to show their dogs. For this show, they'd also joined together to hire a transporter who took the dogs to Colorado Springs, handled their care while at the show, and was supposed to bring them back again."

"Is it common for dog owners to skip shows?" Cole asked. "Seems like it would be important to them."

"The show had events on Friday and Monday and these owners couldn't take time away from work or other commitments," Ellen answered. "They traveled separately for the weekend and hired a transporter for the dogs. They haven't heard from her though."

"Was Rylee the transporter?" Ashley asked.

"Not unless she was using an assumed name," Wendy responded. "None of them knew anyone by the name of Rylee Goodwin."

"Then how did Rylee get the dogs?" Ashley hardly knew what to think. Her unspoken fear that Rylee had stolen the dogs seemed to be confirmed. It was an idea Ashley hadn't wanted to acknowledge, but it was the best explanation for the lack of records and identification for obviously pampered pets.

"Too bad we don't know where she was taking them," Cole said. "Obviously not all the way to Wyoming, since she didn't have any dog food."

"What about her cousin?" Wendy asked. "I know he's a friend of yours, Cole, but are you sure he isn't involved in any way? After all, she was coming here to visit him."

Cole took a moment to answer, and Ashley could see the emotions flitting across his face. Until Josiah's recent move to Aspen Falls, he and Cole hadn't seen much of each other since high school. Their interactions had been sporadic for the past twenty years. A person could change a great deal in two decades, especially in such unstable conditions as Josiah had experienced during his military career.

Cole's expression became stony. "I don't believe it. I *won't* believe it without proof. He was as stunned as the rest of us to see those dogs."

"I don't imagine he'd have booked a room for Rylee at the Lone Elk Bed-and-Breakfast if he'd known," Ashley added. "I doubt the Strattons would have been able to accommodate that many dogs."

Cole shot her a small, grateful smile.

"I'll give Liv a call to be sure." Wendy cleared her throat, then continued in a carefully diplomatic tone, "Forgive me for playing devil's advocate, but it wouldn't have been difficult for Josiah to have kept the dogs at that run-down motel where he's staying. I doubt anyone would have paid much attention to them there."

Cole's lips pressed together, and he shook his head as if trying to dislodge the suspicions that Wendy was planting.

Ashley placed her hand on his arm. "Innocent until proven guilty," she said softly.

Apparently not softly enough. "Of course," Wendy said. "But right now, I have to consider all the possibilities. I am sorry though."

"You're doing your job," Cole said. "I can't begrudge you for that."

"What do the owners want us to do with the dogs?" Ashley asked, as much to change the subject from Josiah's possible involvement in a dog theft as to figure out what plans needed to be made for the dogs' care.

"Holly talked to the folks at Fluffy Friends," Ellen answered. "They're happy to provide all the help we need so the dogs don't have to be crated at the clinic until arrangements can be made to return them to their homes."

"That's great news." Ashley gave quiet thanks for her friend's initiative. "Wendy, do you still want to foster Bridey?"

"Absolutely," the officer said. "I've already talked to Rich, and he's on board."

"Then we only need fosters for the three Brussels and Rugby," Ashley said. "Rugby's X-rays were clear so he can go, but I want Ashes, the sheltie, to stay at the clinic because he's still favoring his leg."

"I'll let Holly know," Ellen said. "Anything else?"

"We're here." Cole flipped on the turn signal and gestured toward the entrance of a long, dirt-packed lane that apparently led to Oscar Moore's house.

"Not right now," Ashley said to the women on the other end of the line. "Thanks so much to both of you. I'll call when we're on our way back."

The call ended, and Ashley shifted her attention to the view outside the windshield. The lane ran between stands of tall pines whose straight trunks and narrowing branches resembled a multitude of church spires. After about a hundred yards, the drive ended in front of a ranch-style house with a detached garage. The landscaping seemed helter-skelter at first glance, with large swathes of native grasses and flowers dominating the property. On closer inspection, though, nothing was overgrown or unkempt. It was simply natural.

A chain-link fence surrounded the house, the garage, and another outbuilding near the rear of the property. A broad porch furnished with chairs, tables, and large potted plants extended from the front of the house, giving it an air of hospitality.

"That could be how Cliffy got away," Cole said as he drove past the open gate and parked near the garage behind a weathered Jeep. Cliffy sat up in the back seat and emitted a low whine. His shoulders and hindquarters trembled. "Hold your horses, fella. We'll let you out in a minute." Cliffy whined again.

Ashley twisted in her seat to observe the dog's body language. Her first reaction had been the same as Cole's—Cliffy was home again and he wanted out. But his vocalization suggested something other than mere excitement. His eyes bulged and his cropped ears were tilted forward. Ashley reached toward him and he licked her fingers, then yawned. He was showing definite signals of stress, though it could be due to the day's strange events.

Or it could be nervousness. Even fear.

Focused on Cliffy's behavior, she replied, "He's been missing for hours. I suppose Mr. Moore might have left the gate open for him, though."

"For all we know, the gate is open all the time." Cole's smile eased her concern, at least a little bit. "Cliffy may come and go as he likes."

"I suppose." Ashley didn't like to judge people based on flimsy evidence, but an unflattering picture of Mr. Moore had already formed in her mind. An unfair picture, perhaps, but it was strange that no one in her sphere of friends—and Cole, Ellen, Ben, and Holly had all lived in town for years—knew much about Cliffy's owner. His property wasn't located that far outside town. She wished she had thought to ask Wendy about him when she was on the phone call with Ellen. "Is he a hermit, do you think?"

"Oscar Moore?" Cole shrugged. "It's possible. We have quite a few eccentric folks around here. If you want to be left alone, these mountains are a great place for it."

"I'm glad that didn't happen for me," Ashley said softly. In the time she'd lived in Aspen Falls, she'd found the best of best friends, a solid support system, and, most important of all, the love of her life.

Cole squeezed her hand. "I'm glad of that too."

For a moment, all of Ashley's concerns about Oscar Moore, Rylee Goodwin, and the stolen show dogs faded away as she lost herself in the depths of Cole's kind green eyes. Until another groan from Cliffy, louder and longer than any of the others, interrupted the tender moment a nanosecond after Cole's lips brushed against hers.

The gentle kiss ended with their lips curving into amused smiles and chuckles.

"It's always going to be this way," Cole said. "If it's not Max coming between us, it's another four-legged interloper."

Ashley chuckled. "Just one of the perks of dating a veterinarian."

"One perk of many." Cole grinned at her, but his mouth fell into a frown as he gazed out the windshield. "Strange that Moore hasn't come out to see who's here."

Ashley agreed. Even though the old-timers still thought of her as a newcomer, she'd been around long enough to know the unwritten protocols and etiquette. Almost anyone else would have been standing on the porch if not already at the Subaru's window.

"Perhaps he has a second vehicle and isn't home," she suggested.

"Only one way to find out." Cole shut off the engine and opened his door. He stood by the front fender, hands on his hips and staring at the house while Ashley slipped a leash on Cliffy and let him out of the vehicle. She wasn't going to take a chance of him running off again before she'd had a chance to talk to his owner.

She joined Cole, and together they headed for the house. Cliffy hurried ahead, practically dragging Ashley, until he reached the four steps leading to the porch. He stared at the screen door then positioned himself behind Ashley, whimpering the entire time.

"Something has him spooked," she told Cole. Not that she could blame him. The property seemed unnaturally quiet.

"Stay here." Cole ascended the steps and knocked on the frame of the screen door. The wooden interior door stood open, providing a glimpse into the house. From her vantage point at the bottom of the steps, Ashley couldn't make out any details.

"Oscar?" Cole called out. "Anyone home?"

Silence. Utter and complete silence.

"Hello?" Cole raised his voice. "Mr. Moore?"

After a moment, Ashley stepped up on the bottom stair. Cliffy stayed where he was, belly on the ground, head between his paws, alternately whimpering and yawning. "What should we do?"

Cole glanced back at her. "Did you notice a doghouse or kennel?"

Ashley scanned as much of the property as she could see. "Maybe he keeps Cliffy in the garage or in that building out back."

"Not in the house?" Before she could answer, Cole stepped

sideways to a large picture window and shaded his eyes to peer inside.

Until she'd witnessed Cliffy's reaction to the house, Ashley would have believed him to be a house dog. His manners at the clinic, even in the break room when the group ate lunch, had been impeccable.

"I don't see much," Cole said. "Normal furniture. But there's a dog bed in front of the fireplace and a doggie door installed in the door at the back of the house."

"So he is a house dog." A finger of fear immediately dampened Ashley's relief. "Then why is he afraid of the house?"

Cole peered around—and his gaze caught on the broad planks of the porch.

"What is it?" Ashley asked.

Cole knelt and studied the boards. "Paw prints." He looked toward Cliffy and back at the boards. "Bloody paw prints."

Ashley stared at Cole, then at Cliffy. She dropped to the ground beside the whimpering dog and wrapped her arm around his broad shoulder. He leaned into her and swiped her chin with his tongue. "What happened in there? Did he hurt you?"

But even as she examined the boxer's paws again and ran her hands over his back and along his chest and stomach, she knew the question didn't make sense. "I can't find any injuries on him. Nothing that would explain the blood on his paws."

"Stay here," Cole said. "I'm going inside."

Ashley's impulse was to go with Cole, but she couldn't leave Cliffy outside by himself. Nor did she want to attempt to make him go inside the house. "Be careful," she said to Cole.

He shot her a quick smile before knocking again on the doorframe. "Mr. Moore, my name is Cole Hawke. I'm a ranger with the Eagle-Holy Cross Ranger District." He paused a moment, then opened the screen door. "I'm here with Dr. Ashley Hart and your dog, Cliffy." He paused again, apparently straining to hear any response. He glanced once more at Ashley. “Mr. Moore, I’m coming inside.”

Ashley stroked Cliffy’s back while focusing on Cole. She held her breath as he stepped across the threshold and disappeared into the interior of the house. “Don’t worry, Cliffy,” she whispered as she stood. “I’m not leaving you.” If only she could see inside the house.

Cole returned a few moments later, pocketing his phone as he came through the door. His grim expression told her something was very wrong. He came to her side, avoiding the bloody paw prints on the porch, and took her hand. When he spoke, his voice was solemn.

“Oscar Moore is dead.”

6

Oscar Moore is dead? Ashley shook her head, knowing she'd heard the words Cole had said but not wanting to believe she'd heard him correctly. "Are you sure? What happened?"

Cole exhaled a deep breath. "I think he was murdered. Chief Maloney is on his way."

"Murdered?" Ashley couldn't control the shiver that racked her body. "Maybe he's still alive. We could administer first aid." She moved toward the house, but Cole blocked her way, pulling her into an embrace.

"It's too late, Ashley. Believe me, if we could have helped him, we would have."

The cottony softness of Cole's T-shirt soothed the sudden heat of her cheek. Though she'd never met the man, the news stunned her and saddened her. Cliffy rose to his feet and pressed his body against their legs. Ashley rested her hand on his head, hoping he was as comforted by her touch as she was by Cole's embrace.

"Think about it," Cole said quietly. "Cliffy had blood on his paws when we found him this morning. If Oscar wasn't already dead by then, he probably died soon after."

"How was he killed?" She braced herself for the answer, though anything Cole said was sure to be awful. Blood almost always meant violence.

"He was stabbed." Cole's arms tightened around Ashley. "There's a knife missing from the butcher block. I didn't look for it."

"That's smart," Ashley said. "You wouldn't want to disturb the crime scene." It was a cardinal rule known by anyone who spent too much time watching police procedurals and detective shows. But it was also a rule that Ashley had become personally familiar with since moving to Aspen Falls, as she'd found herself caught up in more than one grisly murder.

"Though maybe we already have," Cole said.

"How?" Ashley pulled slightly away from him and glanced around the property. Her gaze fell on the Subaru. "Whoever killed him probably drove here."

"Yep," Cole said. "We may have obliterated any tracks."

"What should we do?"

"There's nothing to do but stay put until Chief Maloney gets here." He gestured toward a picnic table situated beneath a large maple tree. "In the shade though."

"Good idea."

Even Cliffy seemed to agree. He trotted alongside Ashley, then curled up under the table at her feet. She and Cole sat across from one another. The table was positioned at an angle to the driveway so they could both see any new arrivals.

Cole had barely sat down when he received a text from Josiah. Rylee's period of consciousness when she was being placed in the ambulance had lasted less than a minute. The physician, Dr. Dennis Quinn, was recommending a CT scan. Cole read the text out loud to Ashley, then showed her his reply before he sent it.

Dr. Quinn is the medical center's director. Rylee is in good hands.

"He said thanks," Cole told Ashley when a text alert beeped again. "I wonder if he knows that Rylee stole the dogs."

"We don't know that for certain," Ashley countered. Though all the evidence so far pointed to that being the case, Ashley was hesitant to accuse the young woman.

"You're right. I wonder if he knows that Rylee *may* have stolen the dogs."

"Should you tell him?"

Cole took a breath. "On one hand, I'd rather he hear the news from me instead of someone else. On the other, I'm not sure it's my place to say anything."

Ashley covered his hand with hers. "Maybe ask Chief Maloney what to do."

"I will," Cole assured her. "If I get the chance."

They sat in companionable silence until faraway sirens broke the stillness, the sound growing louder and louder as police vehicles neared the property. Cliffy crawled from beneath the table, ears pointing forward as he stared at the road.

Two cruisers pulled into the drive and parked behind Ashley's Subaru. Chief Maloney slid out of the first one. Deputy Chief Jana Lewis and Officer Corey Astin emerged from the second.

As Ashley and Cole walked toward the officers, Deputy Chief Lewis tapped on her phone's screen. After initial greetings, she handed her phone to Cole. "We pulled up Oscar Moore's driver's license. Is that the victim?"

Ashley peered over Cole's shoulder as he studied the photo. Though the birth date indicated Oscar was in his midforties, his thick, dark hair showed no traces of gray. His eyes, listed as brown, stared belligerently at the camera.

"It's him." Cole returned the phone.

"Lewis and I will go inside to take a look," Chief Maloney said. "The rest of you stay here. I called for assistance from the state crime lab, and they're on the way."

"*The Avalanche News* is already here." Officer Astin gestured toward the road, where Ed Woodhouse's distinctive Geo Tracker, custom painted a vibrant orange so everyone in Aspen Falls recognized it, had braked to turn into the drive. "He must have been listening to the scanner."

"There's nothing to tell him. Not yet." Chief Maloney stared pointedly at each of them.

Ashley nodded. Her hand rested on Cliffy's head as the dog sat beside her, his shoulder pressed against her leg.

Once the chief was assured that their lips were sealed, he gestured to the property. "Better get the yellow tape around this place, Astin. I don't want anyone on that porch without my say-so."

"Got it, Chief." Officer Astin unlocked his trunk to retrieve the needed materials.

"I'll give you a hand, Corey," Cole volunteered.

While they taped off a large portion of the yard in front of the porch, Ashley explored the property. After all, if she stayed where she was, she'd be the only one for Ed to talk to. Though she liked the amiable owner of the town's newspaper and his wily pet ferret, Archibald, she didn't want to become the source of any of his reporting. Ed was known for his ability to engage in what seemed like a casual conversation that often ended with him finding out exactly what he needed to fill the pages of *The Avalanche News*.

Ashley wandered around to the back of the house, where she found a large garden tucked in one corner against the chain-link fencing. The other two sides of the garden were protected by a three-foot fence. Inside were rows of vegetables, some ready to be picked. Others were in raised beds. In the opposite corner grew a stand of what appeared to be apple trees. There was no doghouse or kennel, so Cliffy likely had the run of the fenced-in area except for the garden. Much of the chain link was covered in flowering vines.

A screened porch and a similar-size deck ran along the rear of the house. Both were comfortably furnished. She allowed Cliffy to lead her to the patio, where he found a chew toy. A sudden breeze ruffled the pages of a paperback book lying on a side table near a gas grill.

Curious what Oscar was reading, Ashley picked up the book and read the cover. *Tryst of Souls* by Ansel Dodger. The author photo on the back wasn't a photo at all, but the profile of a man wearing a black fedora that shadowed half his face. She found the fedora an odd choice for a fantasy writer. Why not a wizard's hat? Either way, it felt too gimmicky to her. Maybe that was another reason she didn't care for Dodger's books.

"Hm," Ashley said to Cliffy. "I didn't think this book had been released yet."

She'd been in the Bookaroo Bookshop the day before to pick up a special order. While she was there, a fortysomething guy wearing a floral shirt with too-short shorts had come in and asked for the latest Ansel Dodger novel. Katee told him her shipment hadn't arrived yet but if he could wait a few days, she might have autographed copies for sale.

The man's mouth had dropped open. "Autographed by Ansel Dodger? He's a known recluse."

"I have a connection," Katee answered with a cryptic smile.

Apparently Oscar had a connection too.

Ashley had read a Dodger novel when it was the Bookaroo Book Club's book of the month. Though the writing was decent and the plot probably had his fans furiously flipping the pages, she preferred novels with more character depth.

She placed the book back on the table as Cole rounded the corner of the house. "There you are," he said. "Find anything interesting out here?"

"Nothing, except that Mr. Moore must have been an Ansel Dodger fan." She pointed toward the book.

"I've read a couple of those novels," Cole said. "They're fun for an escape on a rainy afternoon."

"What's going on in there?" Ashley tilted her head toward the house. "Where's Ed?"

"Hanging around. Hoping to get a word with the chief." Cole sank into a chair as if suddenly weary. "It's almost certain that Mr. Moore was killed with a knife. He has multiple stab wounds, and the knife is missing. We won't know anything for certain until after the autopsy."

"Any word on suspects?"

Cole slowly shook his head. "He was stabbed in the back. I don't think he had a chance to defend himself."

"How awful." Ashley doubted she'd ever get used to the cruelties one human being could inflict upon another. Frankly, she hoped she never did. But that didn't make it any easier to push down the sick feeling churning in her stomach as her imagination played out the scene inside Oscar Moore's home that had ended in his death.

As if sensing her distress, Cliffy padded to her and pushed her hand with his head. She knelt beside him and rested her arm across his back. "What's going to happen to this handsome guy?"

"I guess he'll have to be fostered along with the others," Cole said. "At least until we can find out whether Mr. Moore made any arrangements for his care."

"He can stay with me for a while. Max will enjoy the company."

"That sounds like a good plan." Cole checked his watch. "You should probably go on back to the clinic. I'll catch a ride with Corey."

"You're staying?"

"If nothing else, I can keep Ed occupied until the sheriff is ready to give him a scoop."

Cole and Ashley returned to the front of the house, Cliffy trailing behind them. The police officers were standing by the chief's cruiser with Ed Woodhouse as Officer Astin talked about his first time at a murder scene as a police rookie.

Perhaps that meant the chief had told Ed what he knew about Oscar Moore's death. Still, Ashley decided not to take anything for granted. She'd happily talk to Ed about his ferret, but not about anything else.

The sound of an engine drew their eyes to the road, but the vehicle wasn't yet visible.

"I hope that's the crime lab," Chief Maloney said. "Believe it or not, one of their units was on the way back from a training seminar. They're not that far out of town."

"I hope it's not the big city media." Ed followed his words with a contemptuous grunt. Ed's view, which was common knowledge, was that if the news outlets in Vail and Denver didn't care about the good news coming out of Aspen Falls, then they had no business chasing after the bad.

Cole shaded his eyes as the vehicle rounded a curve and came into sight. "I think it's a mail truck."

"Probably Merle Brooks doing his rounds," Chief Maloney said. "I'm pretty sure his route covers this area."

To their surprise, the mail truck—a modified pickup with a covered bed and the steering setup on the wrong side—didn't stop at the mailbox across from the driveway, but navigated up the lane. It came to a stop near the group, and Merle Brooks slid from the seat. He carried a glass soda bottle that looked like it had just been removed from an ice chest. "What's going on here?" Merle glanced around. "Where's Oscar?"

Chief Maloney ignored both questions. "Why are you here, Merle?"

"I was stopping by on my way back to town to pick up a box of vegetables. Oscar left a note in the mailbox saying he'd have one ready for me." Merle shifted his posture uneasily as if he'd realized that the chief's question wasn't out of idle curiosity. A wary note crept into his voice. "He does that sometimes."

For two or three long seconds, no one spoke. Cliffy had slipped behind Ashley as if to hide from the tension building within the group.

"Oscar's dead," Chief Maloney finally said.

Merle's eyes rounded. and he took a step back. "It was his heart, wasn't it? He complained of chest pains last time I saw him."

"It wasn't his heart," the chief said. "He was murdered."

"M-murdered?" Merle spluttered. "I don't believe it. Who would want to kill Oscar? He never bothered nobody, and ain't nobody ever bothered him."

"He was definitely murdered," Deputy Chief Lewis said, her voice as soft as velvet. "I am sorry for the loss of your friend."

Merle ran a hand over his face, then shook his head. "That doesn't make sense to me. Oscar dead?"

"I'm sorry too," Ashley said. She didn't know Merle all that well, nothing beyond saying hello and discussing the weather or the tourists—what amounted to Aspen Falls small talk when waiting in line at the grocery store or the coffee shop.

The others added their condolences.

"We're expecting the crime lab any minute," Chief Maloney said. "Merle, I'd prefer you not to be here when they arrive. You either, Ashley."

"I'm leaving," she said. "And taking Cliffy with me if that's okay."

"That's fine," Chief Maloney responded. "For the best, frankly."

Ashley smiled her thanks and stepped closer to Cole. She wanted to ask him to bring Cliffy's dog bed, toys, and food back to town if the chief would allow him to do so.

"I'm going too." Merle headed toward his mail truck, but stopped after a couple of steps. "Chief, I don't know if this is important or not. It's probably not, but I just remembered something I found a bit strange."

"We never know what might be important in a case like this," Chief Maloney said.

Merle pointed. "I saw a van pull out of the driveway here when I was a little way up the road this morning. Sped right past me."

"Did you see the driver?" the chief asked.

"It wasn't close enough for that," Merle answered. "It was beige. Older model. Maybe a Dodge."

Ashley caught Cole's gaze and knew his thoughts were the same as hers. Merle had described Rylee's vehicle. Did Josiah's young cousin know something about Oscar's murder? And did it have something to do with why she'd been run off the road?

7

As soon as Ashley walked into the clinic with Cliffy, Max shot out from behind Ellen's desk to greet her. She knelt beside her beloved Dalmatian and welcomed the pressure of his head and neck against her shoulder as she embraced him. The hug didn't last long, though, because once Max realized a new dog had come in, he set about greeting Cliffy with amiable mutual sniffing.

Ellen finished a call, then rested her chin on her folded hands. "You missed Lorie. She and Max got here about fifteen minutes ago. Is it true that Oscar Moore was murdered?"

Ashley frowned. "How could Lorie already know that?"

"Oh, Ashley." Ellen gave her a gentle smile. "Surely you've been here long enough to know the local grapevine is always active." Her face became serious. "So the rumor is true?"

"It's true." Ashley heaved a deep sigh. On the long drive back to town, all she could think about was Merle's description of the vehicle he'd seen leaving Oscar Moore's property. She hoped that Josiah wasn't tapped into the town's gossip grapevine. He didn't need to know that an eyewitness may have placed Rylee at the scene of a murder.

"What about our guests?" she asked Ellen.

"Rich and Andie Heath took Bridey." Ellen held out a printed list. "Fluffy Friends sent over qualified foster homes for the others, including Ashes when you're ready to release him."

Ashley scanned the list naming each dog and its temporary foster family. Gwen Vance, a volunteer for the local adoption and rescue group, and her husband, Adam, the pastor of Faith Church, were fostering Rugby the papillon. Other volunteers, all of whom Ashley knew and trusted, were taking in the griffons.

"Gwen knows about Rugby's tender back," Ellen said before Ashley could ask. The receptionist often guessed what would be on Ashley's mind before she even started to think it. "Do you have a prescription for him?"

"I'll prepare a bottle of pain meds for him before the Three Musketeers get here." Ashley excused herself to get ready for the afternoon's appointments. Max emitted a warbling vocalization, then sauntered back to his fluffy, plaid bed behind Ellen's desk. Cliffy followed Ashley, and she put him in the kennel room, figuring he could use a quiet place to take a nap.

The afternoon at the clinic was busier than Ashley had anticipated. In addition to the scheduled events—including the rambunctious Musketeers—two local teens had found a duck tangled in a fishing line. The line had cut into one of the duck's legs. Fortunately, Ashley and Ben managed to free the bird without putting it under anesthesia. It rested comfortably in the isolation room, though unhappily, judging by its raucous quacks. Ashley didn't want to put it in the same room with Cliffy and Ashes. The teens were coming back the next day in hopes that the duck would have recovered enough for them to return it to where it had been found.

After the clinic closed, Ashley headed home with Max and Cliffy. She grabbed a quick bite to eat while the dogs played in the backyard. Once she had them settled inside her house, she slipped her backpack on her shoulders and rode her bicycle back to the town center for the Bookaroo Book Club meeting. After the long and exhausting day, Ashley reflected that she'd prefer to stay home with the two dogs and a movie, but she was enjoying the club's legal thriller and didn't want to miss the discussion.

As Ashley placed her bike in a rack and looped a chain through the spokes, Holly joined her.

"What a day." Holly exhaled heavily as she tucked a lock of wavy black hair behind her ear. "How'd you manage with the Three Musketeers?"

"Ruby brought three volunteers with her from one of the local 4-H clubs." Ashley chuckled at the memory of the trio of Old English sheepdogs with their young handlers. "We put each of them in a different exam room, then Ruby, Ben, and I went from one to the other. That helped immensely with the chaos."

Holly nodded approvingly. "Clever idea."

"From what I gathered, it counted as a community service project for the kids."

As they stood by the bike rack, Holly bent her head and lowered her voice. "Any updates on the murder?"

Ashley tilted her head. "What do you know?"

Holly's expressive face twisted into a grimace. "Nothing much. It seems Oscar Moore was a bit of a recluse. Though he lived closer to Aspen Falls than Beaver Creek, he did most of his shopping there. And during the summer months, Oscar sold vegetables at the Beaver Creek farmers market. It's a bigger town than ours, so I suppose that makes sense."

The longer Holly talked, the more Ashley's eyes widened. "How do you know all that?"

"My clients." Holly shrugged. "Each one had something to say, and it was rarely the same thing twice. So, I pieced this and that together. The man definitely liked his privacy. I suppose Aspen Falls was too nosy for him."

"I wonder why he would ever think that," Ashley joked.

"I have no idea," Holly said with a laugh.

As the two women strolled past Bookaroo Bookshop's big front window to reach the door, they waved through the glass at the other club members who'd already settled in the cozy reading nook.

"Are we late?" Ashley glanced at her watch. "Nope. We still have several minutes. Why is everyone else so early?"

Holly gently bumped her. "They're not early for the meeting. They're early for the gossip. Prepare yourself for an onslaught of questions."

"Maybe I should have stayed home after all," Ashley muttered.

"And deprive all these people of their fun?" Holly pressed her lips together and shook her head, sending her thick, chin-length waves bouncing. "That's not how things operate in a small town."

"But I can't tell them anything," Ashley protested. "I don't even *know* anything. At least not much."

"But you were there," Holly said. "That's all that matters." She hooked arms with Ashley in a show of solidarity. "Too late to back out now. Let's go."

As Holly predicted, the group showed more interest in Ashley than in the best seller they were there to discuss—everyone except Katee Havenstar, the bookshop's owner and leader of the club, though she appeared more out of sorts than annoyed by the crowd's inattention to the chosen novel. Behind her glasses, her big brown eyes carried a worried expression as if something weighed heavily on her mind. Her usual vivacious personality was tempered by a barely disguised impatience that Ashley had never seen her exhibit before.

Ashley did her best to deter the most persistent questioners by insisting she had no answers for them. "I never went inside the house," and "I left as the crime lab arrived," became her repeated mantras.

The meeting had barely begun when Katee's cell phone buzzed. "Sorry, everyone." She forced a smile, but her eyes deepened with worry. "I have to take this call. Holly, could you please take over the discussion?"

"Sure," Holly readily agreed. "Okay, everyone, what did you think was the most significant red herring in this story?" When one of the members tried to divert the conversation back to Oscar Moore, Holly held up her hand. "Patience, friends. *The Avalanche News* is sure to have all the facts of the case in the morning edition. Isn't that what we all want? Facts instead of fiction?" She smiled her mischievous smile and held up the novel. "Except for this fiction, that is. Now, what was the most significant red herring in the story?"

To Ashley's relief, the group set aside their rumors and speculations to focus on the book. Even so, as soon as the meeting began to wind down, she slipped from her seat and wandered toward the back shelves of the store to avoid any post-meeting gossip about the murder.

The shelves nearest the bookstore's office area held clearance items. Ashley glanced over the merchandise while she retrieved her phone from her backpack. She had no missed calls, but Cole had texted about thirty minutes before to say that he'd stopped in at the medical center to check in with Josiah. Rylee hadn't yet regained consciousness.

Ashley tapped out a brief reply, then peered around the corner to catch a glimpse of the front of the store. A few book club members lingered, either talking with one another or browsing through the stack of new releases. She twisted so she was out of sight and leaned her back against the clearance shelf. The door to Katee's office was slightly ajar. Ashley's senses went on full alert at the sound of muffled sobs.

Was Katee crying?

Ashley bit her lip, said a quick prayer for wisdom, then knocked quietly on the doorframe. "Katee?" she said softly. "It's me, Ashley."

When no response came, she gave the open door a slight push. Katee sat at her desk facing the door and wiping a tissue across her red-rimmed eyes.

Ashley stood in the doorway. "I don't mean to intrude, but if there's anything I can do, please let me know." She let the offer hang in the space between them.

After a moment's hesitation, Katee responded with a weak smile. "It's been one of those days. Nothing's wrong. Really, there isn't."

Ashley wasn't sure she believed Katee, but she didn't want to pry. "I'll go then." She gave Katee a warm smile. "Holly did a great job tonight."

"She managed to get everyone to focus on the book instead of the . . ." Katee waved her hand as if the gesture expressed the word that she couldn't bring herself to say. *Murder*. "I'm impressed."

Glad to see that Katee seemed more like her usual self, Ashley said, "And I was relieved. I don't know the answers to all their questions." She slipped farther into the room. "In fact, that's one reason I came back here. To avoid any more gossip."

Katee gestured toward a chair. "Then have a seat. We'll hide out here together until we get an all clear."

"Are you sure you don't want to be alone?"

Katee tilted her head as if seriously considering the question, then shook her head. "I'd rather have your company. Though you may not want mine."

Ashley gave her a quizzical frown. "Why's that?"

"Because I'm as nosy as anyone else." Katee twisted her features into an exaggerated grimace then became serious. "Could there be a mistake? Maybe Oscar died of natural causes. Or because of an accident."

"I didn't see him," Ashley said, "but Cole did, and so did Chief Maloney. It was definitely murder."

"What about the crime lab? Did you learn anything from them?" Katee's voice trembled, and worry lines furrowed her eyes.

Ashley's nerves tingled. Something about Katee's demeanor made her feel that there was more to the question than mere curiosity. But what could it be?

"The crime lab van arrived as I was leaving," Ashley explained. "In fact, the driver had to wait for me to pull out of the driveway before he could pull in. And not just me. Merle too."

"Merle?" Katee's shoulders stiffened. "You mean the postman?"

"He stopped by to pick up vegetables. Mr. Moore has—I mean, had . . . I mean, his garden is huge. That's why Merle was there."

"Yes, that's true." Katee's voice softened, and her eyes took on a faraway look. "Oscar brought me vegetables sometimes too when I couldn't get to the farmers market."

Ashley's heightened senses relaxed. Was the reason for Katee's unusual behavior, for her unease, simply due to mourning the loss of a friend?

"I'm sure the chief will find out who's responsible," Ashley said, attempting to reassure Katee. But as she said the words, a knot formed in the pit of her stomach.

Katee's gaze sharpened. "Does he already have a suspect?"

Ashley bit her lip. She wanted to support Katee, but not at Rylee's expense.

Katee leaned across the desk, her expression stern. "You know something."

Stunned at Katee's out-of-character confrontational tone, Ashley caved. "Merle saw a vehicle leave Mr. Moore's home this morning," she admitted.

"What kind of vehicle?"

"I can't say any more than that."

Katee's face went white, and she sank back into her chair. "I can't believe Merle saw me," she said, her voice full of despair. She fixed woeful eyes on Ashley. "You have to believe me. I swear I didn't kill Oscar."

8

Before going to the clinic, which opened at eight on Wednesday mornings, Ashley stopped at the medical center. Since she'd left the bookstore the night before, both her heart and mind had struggled with Katee's denial that she'd had anything to do with Oscar's murder. Apparently, Katee believed that Merle had seen her car, which meant she must have been either at Oscar's home or in the vicinity the previous morning.

Even after Ashley reassured her that Merle hadn't described her red sedan—though she didn't share whose vehicle he had described—Katee had refused to tell Ashley whether she'd been at the Moore farm, if she'd seen Oscar before he died, or why she'd be a suspect in his murder.

Ashley couldn't imagine Katee killing anyone, but she'd learned that sometimes the most unlikely person could be capable of the most horrifying deeds. She almost wished she had never entered Katee's office, and she definitely regretted mentioning Merle.

None of her efforts to calm Katee's fears had helped. When Holly had appeared in the office doorway, Katee had pasted on a vibrant smile and shooed both of them out in an over-the-top good-natured way that had fooled no one.

As she entered the medical center, Ashley did her best to put aside her concern for Katee so she could focus on Josiah. Since Cole had to be at the ranger station early that morning, he'd called last night and asked her to check on his friend, who refused to leave the medical center.

Ashley found Josiah in the tiny cafeteria, pushing scrambled eggs, sausage links, and hash browns around on his plate. The cliché of horrible hospital food didn't hold true in Aspen Falls. Ashley knew that a few residents went to the medical center for takeout. Josiah's lack of interest in his meal and his bent head indicated his worried mood.

"Mind if I sit down?" Ashley asked.

Josiah lifted his gaze to hers. The sadness in his eyes pressed against her. When he started to rise from his chair, she motioned for him to stay seated.

"Please do." He gestured toward the seat across from him. "Can I get you anything? The food is—" He waved his hand over his plate, then his face clouded. "To be honest, I can't even tell you whether it's good or not."

"Thanks, but I'm fine." Ashley settled in her chair. "Cole said he offered for you to crash at his place. Why don't you go there and get some rest?"

"I can't leave her." Josiah placed the fork on his plate and folded his hands. "When she wakes up, I need to be here."

"What about her parents?"

"Her dad moved away after the divorce and has never been seen again." Josiah released a heavy sigh. "I left a message for her mom, but who knows if she'll call back. She's a bit flighty."

Maybe that's where Rylee gets it. "Sounds like Rylee had a tough childhood."

"Yeah. My parents did what they could, but . . ." He shrugged. Regret seemed to envelop him. "I suppose that's why Rylee has always had a heart for the underdog." One side of Josiah's mouth quirked up as if he didn't know whether to frown or smile. "She knows what it's like to be vulnerable, so she listens to anyone with a sob story. People take advantage of her, but she never sees it that way. Instead, she only sees the so-called 'injustice.' One month it's protesting turkey shoots, the next it's boycotting gasoline. Though that one didn't last long, considering she needs gas for her own car."

"Do you think that was what happened here?" Ashley asked. "Though I can't imagine any reason to take show dogs from their owners. They're all healthy and well-adjusted."

Josiah's eyes widened. "Are you saying she stole those dogs?"

Ashley's heart fell to her stomach as her mind stumbled over how to respond. Cole must not have had the chance to tell him yet, or perhaps Chief Maloney had advised Cole not to say anything to his friend. Both of which were scenarios that Ashley should have remembered before saying what she had.

"I don't believe it." The stern set of Josiah's features reminded Ashley of the determined expression he'd worn while riding his bike up the steep mountain path. "Why would anyone think she'd do such a thing?"

"There could be some mistake," Ashley said, trying to reassure him.

"Except?"

Ashley bit her lip and glanced away. Though she wasn't sure it was her place to tell him why Rylee was a suspect, she also believed he had a right to know. She took a deep breath as she made her decision. "All the dogs' owners live around Amarillo, Texas. They hired someone, a transporter, to take the dogs to and from a weekend show in Colorado Springs."

"You're telling me that Rylee was supposed to take the dogs back to Amarillo?" Josiah narrowed his eyes in confusion. "Then why was she bringing them north?"

"That's just it. They didn't hire Rylee." Ashley sighed. "None of the owners have ever heard of her."

When Josiah hung his head, Ashley sat in silence, wishing she knew what to say to alleviate his distress. Then again, sometimes silence was the best gift one person could give another.

A few moments later, Josiah raised his head, but he avoided eye contact. "I've bailed her out of jail a couple times." He shifted in his seat and a rueful smile crossed his lips. "Nothing too serious. Trespassing. Vandalism. Both times she completed her community service, even seemed to enjoy her sentencing because she was doing something good." He faced Ashley. "I thought she'd grow out of causing trouble and find better ways to effect change. That she'd realize there are multiple sides to any important issue, and her criminal behavior did more harm than good."

"Is that why you think she took the dogs?" Ashley asked. "To right some wrong?"

As a veterinarian, Ashley had some insight into the competitive world of dog conformation, in which owners or their handlers competed to see whose dog came closest to matching the breed standard. First, each dog went up against the other dogs of the same breed, usually by age groups, then the age group winners competed against each other. The winners of each breed, who received points toward a championship title, then competed for the Best in Group—the hounds against other hounds, terriers against other terriers, and so on. The winners of each group then competed for the Best in Show title.

Ashley worked with a handful of show dogs at Happy Tails, all of whom were healthy and happy. However, she didn't approve of breed clubs that focused on the exaggeration of a few physical traits while ignoring overall health considerations. When a dog's muzzle became so flat it affected the breathing, she thought that was wrong. She felt the same when a dog was built with such a heavy bone structure that it could no longer be naturally impregnated or safely deliver puppies without an operation. Fortunately, many breed clubs now tested for common ailments such as hip dysplasia and eye issues to eradicate these defects from their lines and to produce healthier litters.

"I don't know what to think," Josiah said, finally answering Ashley's question. "What possible reason could Rylee have to take dogs that didn't belong to her?"

"We haven't heard her side of the story yet," Ashley reminded him. "This could all be some misunderstanding."

"I hope she gets the chance to tell it." Josiah's eyes, already red from lack of sleep, grew watery. He closed them and pinched the bridge of his nose.

Ashley wished she knew how to help him. She scanned the cafeteria as if seeking an answer, and caught sight of Chief Maloney as he entered. She waved her hand in greeting, and he maneuvered past the other tables toward them.

As the chief approached, Josiah rose from his seat and the two men shook hands. Ashley gathered her belongings. "I'll give you some privacy."

"I'd like for you to stay, Ashley," Josiah urged. "I could use a friend right now."

"Sure," Ashley agreed. "If the chief doesn't mind."

"It's probably for the best," Chief Maloney said. "Besides, I'd rather you hear this from me too, instead of through the town's grapevine."

"What's happened?" Ashley asked.

"The van that Rylee was driving was reported stolen yesterday. The owner, Valerie Nelson, says she stopped at a rest area near Pueblo and left the vehicle running because the dogs were inside. She was only gone a few minutes, but when she returned, the van was gone."

"You believe Rylee stole the van?" Josiah shook his head. "I don't understand why she'd do something like that. Or why she was bringing those dogs here." His eyes widened as he stared at Chief Maloney.

"You don't think I have anything to do with this, do you?"

"I don't want to believe that," Chief Maloney said. "If there's anything you can tell us about your cousin and her possible involvement with these dogs, now is the time."

"We were supposed to go out for dinner," Josiah said. "She was staying the night at the Lone Elk. Then, as far as I knew, she was driving on to Wyoming for a job." His shoulders slumped. "I wish I could tell you something—give you a reason to believe this is a big misunderstanding. But I don't know. We won't know until she wakes up."

Chief Maloney held Josiah's gaze a moment, then shifted to Ashley. "Did you tell him about Oscar Moore?"

Ashley shook her head, thankful that she hadn't blurted out anything about the murder or what Merle Brooks, the postman, had told them the day before.

"Who's Oscar Moore?" Josiah asked.

"The owner of the boxer we found," Ashley said.

"What boxer?"

"Oh, that's right. He showed up after the ambulance left," Ashley explained. "It was another dog, but we found out that he belonged to someone local. Oscar Moore."

"Belonged?" Wariness crept into Josiah's tone. "As in past tense?"

Chief Maloney adjusted his glasses, his blue eyes serious. "When Ashley and Cole went out to his place yesterday to return his dog, they discovered Mr. Moore's body. He'd been murdered."

Josiah's face paled beneath his tan. "Murdered?" he croaked. "What does that have to do with Rylee?"

"What makes you think it has anything to do with Rylee?" Chief Maloney asked, his tone even.

"I've investigated enough military crimes to understand interrogation techniques," Josiah said. "The most likely reason for you to bring this up is because you suspect Rylee. But just because she stole that van—and we don't know with full certainty that she did—that doesn't mean she had anything to do with Oscar Moore."

"You're right," Chief Maloney said. "Except that we have an eyewitness who saw a vehicle matching the description of the stolen van at Mr. Moore's home yesterday morning. And the accident took place on the route almost anyone would take from Mr. Moore's place into town."

"Who's the eyewitness?" As soon as the words were out of his mouth, Josiah waved his hand as if erasing them. "Never mind. I know you can't tell me that."

"Not yet," Chief Maloney said. "Though I'm sure it'll be all around town before nightfall."

"I don't believe Rylee killed anyone," Josiah protested. "I can't believe it."

"I know this is a difficult time for you," Chief Maloney said. "I'd appreciate it, though, if you could drop by the station sometime later today and provide an official statement."

Josiah pressed his lips together before agreeing. "I can do that."

"I'll go then." The chief stood and nodded goodbye.

Once Chief Maloney was gone, Ashley leaned forward. "I'm so sorry, Josiah."

"She didn't do it," he said, his voice filled with a confidence Ashley wasn't sure he actually felt. "She couldn't."

"Maybe it was whoever was riding the motorcycle that she said was trying to run her off the road. Maybe Rylee saw something she shouldn't have." Those were the only words Ashley had to reassure him. Of course Josiah didn't want to believe his cousin was capable of murdering another human being, but the chief must think the evidence pointed to Rylee. Merle's eyewitness testimony placed her at the scene. Cliffy's presence at the accident site made it look as if she'd taken him too.

Except Cliffy had had Oscar's blood on his paws, and if he'd been put in the van right after the murder, he'd have left prints inside the vehicle. Ashley made a mental note to ask Chief Maloney if Oscar's blood had been found in the van. She doubted the crime lab had that information yet since they'd gathered the evidence the day before. Even if the chief requested a rush on the evidence, it could be days, even weeks, before they got any results. It was just as likely, if not more so, that Cliffy had wandered away from his property and ended up at the accident site with the other dogs.

Josiah grew more agitated. "He suspects me too."

"No way," Ashley said firmly.

"Rylee was coming to see me. Driving a stolen van full of stolen dogs." His fist smacked the table, causing the silverware to clatter. "I'd suspect me if I were in his shoes."

Josiah closed his eyes and took a couple of deep cleansing breaths. The calming technique appeared to work. When he opened his eyes, they were still red, but clear of any of his earlier doubt and worry.

"I was a criminal investigator," he said. "And if it's the last thing I do, I'm going to clear Rylee's name and mine. I'm innocent, and I know she is too."

"Josiah," Ashley began but he held up a hand to cut her off.

"She's no murderer. And I'll do whatever I have to do to prove that."

Without another word, he gathered his dishes, dropped them at a busing station against the wall, and strode from the cafeteria. His resolve was apparent from the set of his shoulders and the purpose in his steps. He was a man on a mission, and Ashley felt a tremor of fear for anyone who got in his way.

9

The last patient of the day, an adorable silver and white mini-lop rabbit with an upper respiratory infection called pasteurellosis, rested in Ben's arms while Ashley injected an antibiotic into the rabbit's mouth. "That should fix his snuffles," she said as she disposed of the syringe, then handed Ben a bag containing more syringes to be given orally, as well as antibiotic eye drops to help clear the infection. "Especially combined with these."

"Got it," Ben said before he disappeared into a nearby exam room to deliver the lop-eared bunny to its ten-year-old owner.

Ashley glanced at the wall clock as she washed her hands. Though it was only three o'clock, she was exhausted. Ben had volunteered to close the clinic, and she'd gladly agreed. Her other part-time veterinary assistant, Jen Lockwood, would be by after hours to take Ashes, the sheltie, home with her for the night. His leg seemed much better, but he needed more opportunities to exercise than he was getting in the clinic.

Since she had no farm calls scheduled, all Ashley needed to do was to put her final notes on the rabbit in the computer, get leashes on Max and Cliffy, drive home, and collapse on her couch.

Cole had church choir practice that night, but he'd said that he might come over afterward for an evening snack unless he went to the hospital to spend time with Josiah. Perhaps she should suggest he do that instead. She hadn't yet had a chance to talk to him about Josiah's reaction to Chief Maloney's visit that morning. Whenever she had a free moment, Cole was tied up with his own duties. When he'd returned her calls, she'd been unable to answer.

Such was their life on a good day. When there was a murder to solve, it was even harder for them to connect.

As Ashley finished the entry and closed the records program, Ellen entered the prep area. "There's a woman here," she said in a low voice. "Valerie Nelson. She's come for the dogs."

"Chief Maloney mentioned her name this morning when I was at the medical center with Josiah." Ashley frowned. "You mean she's here for the show dogs?"

"She says she has all the necessary paperwork giving her responsibility for them, but . . ." Ellen bit her lip.

"What is it?"

"I'm not sure. She's polite enough, but there's something off about her." Ellen shrugged, and a small smile tugged at the corner of her mouth. "What can I say? I don't trust her."

Ashley slid off the stool she'd been sitting on and placed a hand on Ellen's arm. "I trust your instincts."

Ellen held out a folded sheet of paper. "The names of the owners and their dogs are listed here. Savannah Drake, who owns the Cavalier spaniel, called earlier. She confirmed the names and said she'd be here Friday to pick up all the dogs."

Ashley scanned the paper. "I don't see Valerie Nelson's name on this list."

"That's because none of those dogs belong to her." Tension edged Ellen's normally calm voice. "She said she was hired to transport them."

"Is anyone else still here?"

"Ben is sitting at the front desk."

Ashley blew out air while her mind raced with possible scenarios. But there was one logical thing for her to do, and that was wait for

Savannah Drake, a legal owner, to show up and give her possession of the dogs. They had been stolen once, and Ashley wouldn't hand them over to a stranger now. For all she knew, Valerie Nelson could be an accomplice in the original theft. Or maybe she was the thief, and Rylee had taken the dogs from her. Could that be the reason Rylee had stolen the van?

"What should we do?" Ellen asked.

"I should stop letting my imagination run away with me," Ashley replied with a smile. When Ellen gave her a quizzical look, Ashley chuckled. "Never mind. I'll check out Ms. Nelson's paperwork, but those dogs are staying with their foster families until Ms. Drake arrives and we're assured of the other owners' wishes."

"I think that's wise," Ellen said. "Do you think I'm being paranoid if I contact Fluffy Friends and warn them that someone may be searching for the dogs, and the foster families should contact us before they hand over any of the dogs to a stranger?"

"More cautious than paranoid, I'd say," Ashley reassured her. "Go ahead and call them. I'll talk to Ms. Nelson."

The woman in the reception area appeared to be in her midtwenties. Her shoulder-length hair had been stripped of color except for an inch-wide brunette band at her roots. Extra-long false lashes framed her large brown eyes. Purple hues shaded her eyelids, while bright blush and lip color clashed instead of enhancing her natural prettiness.

"I'm Valerie Nelson," she said as Ashley entered. Her overly warm smile didn't reach her eyes. "You must be the veterinarian who found my dogs. I'm here to take them home."

"It's nice to meet you." Ashley returned the smile. Like Ellen, she sensed a falseness in Valerie's demeanor. "I'm sorry you didn't call before coming all this way. I would have told you that none of the owners have given me permission to hand their dogs over to you."

"You've been in contact with the owners?" Valerie's tone took on a hard edge.

"Naturally. All the dogs were microchipped, so it didn't take long to identify them."

"No, it wouldn't have." Valerie stared at Ashley as if sizing her up, then smiled again as she pulled a folder from her oversize bag. "This is the contract I have with the handler who was responsible for the dogs during the Colorado Springs competition. Acting as the legal representative for each of the owners, he hired me to transport the dogs to Amarillo. Unfortunately, and as I'm sure you're aware"—her voice caught, and she blinked her heavily made-up eyes as if to stop herself from crying—"my vehicle was stolen." She lowered her head as if overcome with emotion at the memory. "I can't tell you how upsetting it was to come out and find them all gone. They are all such valuable dogs, and I only left them for a few minutes. And then I found out my van was wrecked. It's all been too much. Just too much."

Ashley exchanged glances with Ellen and Ben, who seemed as unimpressed as she felt.

"We were surprised that there wasn't any paperwork in the vehicle." Ashley opened the folder Valerie had handed her. Inside, a single sheet of paper indicated that Ms. Valerie Nelson was to be paid a designated amount of money to transport the dogs to and from the competition in Colorado Springs and their Amarillo homes. The document listed the name and breed of each dog along with the corresponding owner's name and address.

"I had the paperwork with me," Valerie said. "In my bag."

Before Ashley could respond, Ben piped up. "Why weren't any of the dogs wearing collars?"

Valerie faced him, eyes narrowed as if offended by his question. But her displeasure quickly disappeared behind a false mask of surprised innocence. "That's strange. They all had collars on when I left them in the van."

"We thought it strange too," Ashley said, her tone as nonchalant as she could make it. Runaway imagination or not, she agreed with Ellen. Something wasn't right about this woman. Ashley trusted Ellen's instincts even if she sometimes doubted her own. No way was Valerie Nelson leaving Aspen Falls with even one of the show dogs, let alone all of them. Not to mention the fact that Valerie's van wasn't fit to drive. How did she expect to transport them?

"Perhaps the thief got rid of them," Valerie said. "Though why anyone would steal them to begin with—it's horrible to even think about. I can't imagine why anyone would do such a thing. Can you?"

Valerie's tone caused Ashley to raise her eyes from the document. The question was a simple one, and yet it almost sounded as if Valerie was testing her. Or giving her an opportunity to guess at a motive.

"Perhaps to sell them," Ashley suggested. Though the reward was hardly worth the risk. But had that been Rylee's plan?

"I suppose." Valerie's face brightened as she flashed a huge smile. "May I see the dogs now? I'm sure you've done everything you can for them, being a vet and all, but I'm anxious to see them for myself. They're all gorgeous, aren't they?"

"They're beautiful," Ashley replied. "But they're not here."

Valerie's features darkened, and her shoulders stiffened. "Where are they?"

Ashley tilted her head as if in thought while she settled on an appropriate answer that wouldn't be a lie. "Elsewhere."

"What does that mean?"

"It means they aren't here."

Valerie's tone grew cold. "You've seen the contract. Those dogs are my responsibility, and their owners are eager for their return."

Without asking for permission, Ashley made a copy of the document, then handed the original to Valerie, whose hand shook as she took it.

"I have no idea if this is a valid contract," Ashley said. "Even if it is, it's between you and the handler. There's nothing that says the owners want you to pick up their dogs for them now. That's the kind of documentation I need to release the dogs to you."

Ashley wasn't sure why she didn't tell Valerie that one of the owners was on her way to Aspen Falls. That would be the easy way out, but for once she had no doubt in her instincts, which were telling her to keep that information to herself. In her view, the less information Valerie had about the dogs, their current whereabouts, and the arrangements being made for their return, the better for all concerned.

"I see," Valerie said, her tone now as smooth as silk. "Do you have an attorney, Dr. Hart?"

Ashley's stomach knotted at the unexpected question. "I do." *His name is Hector Slade, and his law offices are upstairs.*

"That's good." Valerie arched her eyebrow as she thrust the folder into her bag. "You'll be hearing from mine." Without another word, she pivoted on her heel and stomped out.

When the door closed, Ashley realized that she'd been holding her breath. She slowly released it.

"Wow." Ben tapped his cell phone. "I recorded everything she said."

"I'm not sure that's legal," Ashley responded, though she was glad that he had.

Ellen held out her phone so Ashley and Ben could see the numbers *911* on the screen. "All I had to do was hit send."

Ashley dropped into a nearby chair, suddenly feeling as if her feet couldn't hold her another moment. "You two are the best."

"Of course we are," Ellen replied as she shooed Ben from her desk. "I'm going to call Savannah Drake and ask her about this Valerie Nelson."

"Thank you, Ellen," Ashley said. "I'll be interested in knowing what she has to say."

"What if Valerie finds out who has the dogs?" Ben asked. "It wouldn't be hard. Everyone in town knows."

"You're right," Ellen agreed. "I'll call the foster families and give them a heads-up before I talk to Fluffy Friends. Now Ashley, you take Max and Cliffy home and get some rest before any emergency calls come in."

Ashley slowly rose to her feet, gathered her belongings and the dogs, and made the short drive to her log cabin home. She changed into shorts and a tank top, then took the dogs outside. She lounged in a cushioned glider while Max and Cliffy chased each other around the backyard.

Ellen's text arrived soon after. *SD says VN is legit, but owners agree SD is to get dogs. Confirmed she's driving here on Friday.*

Ashley thanked her, then mulled over the information. Perhaps she owed Valerie an apology for being suspicious. The woman's odd behavior may have been out of fear that her reputation as a responsible transporter would be ruined by the theft of the dogs. Who would want to hire someone to transport their valuable dogs when other dogs had been stolen from that person's care?

Ashley regretted that she hadn't been kinder to Valerie. Instead, she'd let her own paranoia affect her usually good judgment. Instead of being evasive, she could have asked Ellen to call Savannah while Valerie was at the office. That one phone call would have been enough to settle the issue, and there would have been no mention of attorneys.

Though Valerie could also have called Savannah or one of the other owners. Why had she made a threat instead of a phone call?

Ashley replayed the conversation in her mind as well as she could remember, but she couldn't pinpoint anything that stood out as especially suspicious. Again, she went back to her own actions, her own cautious evasiveness that may have fed into Valerie's insecurities.

Except there was something about her. Both Ashley and Ellen couldn't be wrong. Even Ben, who saw the best in everybody, had been on guard.

There was nothing more she could do now. Tomorrow was another day and all that. And on Friday, Savannah Drake would arrive. She'd take the dogs to their owners. And maybe, hopefully, Rylee Goodwin would wake from her coma and tell them what had happened.

Why she'd been driving a stolen van. Why she'd been at Oscar Moore's house.

Why he'd been murdered.

10

The clinic didn't open until two on Thursdays, but Ashley had a handful of farm calls to make before heading back to town. Since none of the calls were emergencies, she scheduled the farm that was farthest from town first and the closest one last.

Though the day was drenched in sunshine and fluffy clouds rested on the mountains—one of her favorite kind of days for driving around the countryside—Ashley started her morning feeling out of sorts after a restless night's sleep punctuated with dreams of bullets hitting a van, injured dogs, and a young woman's plaintive cries. "It's all my fault. I didn't mean it. It's all my fault."

Ashley snoozed her alarm when it went off. At least she thought she did. Instead, she apparently shut off the alarm. Half an hour later, when she awoke to Max's low whine, she felt discombobulated and uncharacteristically cranky. Apparently the extra sleep hadn't done her much good.

While the dogs went out for their morning sniffs, she got dressed and brewed a pot of coffee. Jen sent a quick text saying that Ashes had done great and that she'd drop him off at the clinic later in the day. The news cheered Ashley's spirits, and she left on her farm rounds, to-go mug in hand, in a much better mood.

The first call went well. A well-to-do couple wanting to acquire a new pony for their kids had asked Ashley to check out two possibilities. Such a request was rare but not unheard of, and Ashley had built up a rapport with the family when she'd cared for their other beloved pets.

Both ponies she met were used to children and had good temperaments. When they passed their health exams with flying colors, the parents found it difficult to choose the best one. They left it to the children to decide, but the kids were divided in their choice. Unable to pick one of the sweet ponies, the family bought both.

Ashley stayed around while the ponies were loaded into the family's horse trailer and driven away. The seller then asked her to evaluate two other ponies who weren't quite as docile as the first ones. They were every bit as healthy, though.

As Ashley drove to her second appointment, she passed a mail truck. When the driver pressed the horn, Ashley glanced in her rearview mirror. Merle Brooks stuck his head out his window and waved frantically.

Ashley maneuvered her Subaru to the side of the road and rolled down her window. Sun-warmed air flowed into the air-conditioned interior as the mail truck pulled up beside her.

"What are you doing out this way?" Merle's voice boomed cheerfully.

"Farm calls," Ashley replied.

"You do those a lot?"

"As many as need to be done, usually on Tuesday and Thursday mornings. And, of course, whenever there's an emergency."

"I'm glad I ran into you." Merle rested his arm on top of his open window and leaned out. "I've been wondering about Oscar's dog. You took him with you when you left his place the other day."

"I couldn't very well leave him there." Ashley hadn't meant to sound defensive, but she couldn't help it. Maybe her earlier crankiness hadn't gone away after all. "Chief Maloney said it was okay."

"What did you do with him?" Merle asked.

Under other circumstances, Ashley wouldn't have thought twice about answering such a question. Sure, it was a little on the nosy side—okay, a *lot* on the nosy side—but nosy questions were typical in a small town like Aspen Falls. Plus, the answer was a simple one. When it came to the boxer, she certainly didn't have anything to hide.

And yet something about Merle's tone, which didn't come across as disinterested as she believed he intended, gave her the same feeling she'd experienced when Valerie Nelson had arrived at the clinic eager to take possession of the show dogs.

"Why do you ask?" Ashley was almost as surprised by her question as the postman seemed to be.

His expression quickly transformed from surprise to a feigned indifference. "No special reason, except that Oscar thought the world of that dog. I'd sure hate to see him end up in a shelter."

"That won't happen," Ashley assured him.

"Glad to hear it." Merle pressed his lips together while he nodded, as if Ashley had said something especially wise. "It may be too soon to say it, but I wouldn't mind giving him a home should he need one."

Ashley's mind raced to come up with an appropriate response. Between work, concerns about the show dogs, and Oscar's murder, she hadn't given much thought to what would happen to Cliffy. Perhaps Oscar had a will that gave instructions about the dog's care or at least named an executor who was responsible for making such a decision.

If Oscar hadn't made any arrangements, then Ashley would likely place him with Fluffy Friends Adoption and Rescue. They were best equipped to find the perfect home for the fun-loving boxer. If Merle Brooks was serious, she'd let him know, but he'd still have to fill out an application with the organization.

"Do you know if Mr. Moore left instructions for him?" she asked. "If he had an attorney?"

"We never talked about anything like that. Keep me in mind when you start looking for a home. The wife and I will take as fine care of him as Oscar did. Maybe even better." The mail truck lurched forward as if to move along, then stopped again. "Don't suppose you know if the crime lab came up with anything?"

"It's probably too soon for that," Ashley replied. "But even if they did, I wouldn't know what they found out."

"I got the impression you have an in with the chief. Thought he might pass along the news."

The conversation was making Ashley feel more and more uncomfortable. She couldn't easily move her Subaru with the mail truck parked on the road beside her, but she was anxious to leave.

"Chief Maloney hasn't told me anything," she said lightly in hopes that would end Merle's questions.

"No, I don't suppose he would." The vehicle inched forward again. "I'd better get going. Folks are expecting their mail, rain or shine, hail or sleet, and all that."

Ashley smiled at the allusion to the post office's informal motto. "The same goes for veterinarians."

"Guess that's true too. See you around, Dr. Hart." Without waiting for a reply, Merle checked his mirrors and headed for the next house.

Ashley mulled over the conversation with Merle as she drove to her next farm call. It had been unsettling, though Ashley couldn't explain why. What had he done except offer to provide a home for a homeless boxer and ask a couple gossipy questions? He wasn't the only one, she reminded herself. *Think of all the questions I had to dodge at book club Tuesday night.* Everyone in town was curious about what had happened to Oscar, and with good reason. Someone had killed the man. Until the killer was caught, no one could rest easy.

Although the clinic was open until seven on Thursdays, the last appointment left before five. With such a light schedule for the day, Ellen hadn't come in. Naturally, Ashley would stay at the clinic until closing, but no one else needed to. Both Ben and Jen lived close enough that Ashley could call them in case of any emergencies.

Alone in the clinic, Ashley removed the gate she'd set up in the break room doorway to restrict the big dogs' movements. Max usually had free run of the place even during office hours. He liked to nap behind Ellen's desk, hang out with Ashley in her office, or watch Ben and Jen work in the large prep area.

But Max and Cliffy together could be overwhelming, especially for Ashley's more nervous clients. Plus, she wasn't completely confident in how Cliffy would react to other animals. He seemed friendly enough, but he hadn't been vetted as thoroughly as Max. The break room was large enough to give the two dogs plenty of space to nap and stretch their legs.

Ashley fed the two dogs their supper, then took a bowl of food to Ashes. The sheltie whimpered as she opened the cage door.

"You can come out to eat, sweet boy," she said softly. "I know it's not fun to be cooped up, but you won't have to do this much longer. Jen will come back for you this evening, and someone will be here tomorrow to take you home."

Ashley sat on the floor, legs crossed, while Ashes daintily ate his food. He was about halfway through when the buzzer rang, alerting her that someone had come in the front door.

"It's me," Cole called. "And Josiah."

Ashley rose to her feet, but in the two seconds it took her to leave the kennel room, Max and Cliffy were already racing each other toward the entrance.

"Incoming!" Ashley shouted. "Come on back when you can."

She stood in the doorway between the kennel room and the large prep area to keep an eye on Ashes, who was distracted by all the commotion he could hear but couldn't see. "Finish your dinner," Ashley urged.

Cole and Josiah appeared in the prep area with the two big dogs prancing around their legs. Cole held up two carryout bags. "We brought supper. Hope you're hungry."

"Sure am." Ashley tipped her head toward Ashes. "Just waiting for this little slowpoke to finish his dinner."

Cole placed the bags on a nearby counter, then pecked Ashley on the cheek. "How's he doing?" he asked, nodding toward the sheltie.

"His leg is still sore, but he's getting around better every day. And his appetite is definitely improving." She gently elbowed Cole's ribs. "When he's not distracted by unexpected visitors." She smiled at Josiah. "It's good to see you outside of the hospital. Any news?"

Josiah's lips curved upward into a weak smile. "Rylee opened her eyes this afternoon. But for less than a minute. She tried to say my name before she slipped under again. At least, I think that's what she was trying to say."

"That has to be a good sign." Ashley inwardly gave thanks for the small stepping-stone. Hopefully it meant Rylee was on the mend and would regain full consciousness soon.

"It's an answer to my prayers," Josiah agreed as Cliffy pressed against his shins. "This must be the boxer you were telling me about."

"Josiah, meet Cliffy," Ashley joked. "Apparently your new best friend."

Josiah's earlier attempt at a smile transformed into a genuine one as he knelt beside the boxer. "You doing okay, buddy? Life been kind of hard the past couple of days?"

Ashley wasn't entirely sure whether Josiah was asking Cliffy or himself. One thing was certain. Cliffy already adored Josiah and didn't want so much as a molecule to separate them. She leaned closer into

Cole while wishing she could do more for Josiah and Rylee.

"I had a boxer when I was a kid," Josiah said as Cliffy practically knocked him over. "Best dog ever."

"Cliffy is great too," Ashley said. "Well-behaved and fun to have around."

"I can see that." Josiah endured another chin licking, then stood while gently rubbing Cliffy's silky ear between his fingers. "What's going to happen to him?"

"I need to find out if Mr. Moore made any arrangements for him," Ashley said. "Until then, he'll stay with me."

"Whoever gets him will be lucky," Josiah said.

"Are you interested?" Cole asked.

Josiah gazed at the boxer, who remained pressed against his leg. "Maybe, after all this with Rylee gets settled. If it ever does."

"It will," Ashley reassured him. "What did Dr. Quinn say about her progress?"

"He said it was a good sign that she recognized me." Josiah gave a rueful smile. "Then he told me to go away for a while. So I went biking and now I'm here, joining you and Cole for supper. Exactly what you wanted, right? A third wheel."

"You're never that." Ashley grinned at Cliffy. "I'm obviously not the only one who's glad you're here."

Josiah bent to pat Cliffy's shoulder again. "He does seem taken with me, doesn't he?"

Ashley smiled her agreement, though she also found Cliffy's reaction interesting. The boxer was showing more genuine affection with Josiah than he had with anyone else. Strange how an animal sometimes "took" to a specific person, as if the two had a kind of special, invisible bond. She'd seen it often during her years of practice, but no one had ever been able to explain it.

"Okay if I set up supper in the break room?" Cole asked.

"Please do," Ashley replied. "I'll join you in a minute."

Cliffy and Max trailed the two men to the break room. Ashley spent a few moments loving on Ashes, then tidied up the area. As she did so, she thought about Ashes's long drive back to Amarillo with Savannah.

"How can I make you comfortable for such a long trip?" she murmured as she stroked the sheltie's thick coat. "I know you'll feel so much better once you're home." A reunion was perhaps the best medicine the sweet little dog could receive.

Too bad Ashley didn't have it in her clinic pharmacy.

She entered the break room to find Cole and Josiah seated at a table covered in food and utensils. Max raised his head, but she held up her hand in a stay command. He made a warbling noise before resting his nose on his outstretched paws. Cliffy sprawled halfway beneath the table with one paw possessively on Josiah's boot.

Cole rose and pulled out a chair for Ashley. "We brought tonight's special from Icebreakers Pub. You've got a choice between lasagna, lasagna, and lasagna. Salads and breadsticks included."

"Oh, fun. Italian night." Ashley hadn't realized how hungry she was until the aromas had tantalized her nostrils. Though no wonder. She'd only eaten a granola bar and a banana when she arrived at the clinic after her farm calls. "It all smells so delicious, I don't know how to decide. I guess I'll take lasagna."

They chatted about nothing of importance while they ate. Josiah kept his phone nearby so he wouldn't miss a call and occasionally gave Cliffy meat from his lasagna when he thought Ashley and Cole weren't watching. Ashley usually didn't approve of feeding dogs from the table, but after the recent traumas both the man and the dog had experienced, she didn't have the heart to reprimand them.

When Josiah finished his meal, he crumpled up his napkin and placed it in the to-go container. "I've got something I need to tell you," he said. "Chief Maloney gave me a call before I left the hospital. It's not good news."

Ashley exchanged a glance with Cole, but his expression told her that he didn't know about the call. Both turned their attention to their friend, giving him time and space to tell them what the chief had said in his own way.

Josiah took a long sip of his sweet tea, then he folded his arms on the table. He started to speak, stumbled, cleared his throat, and tried again. "The lab found Oscar Moore's blood on Rylee's shirt."

"Her shirt?" Ashley echoed. "Oh, Josiah. I'm so sorry."

"I don't want to believe she killed him." Josiah's voice trembled, and he cleared his throat again. "The Rylee I know would never do such a thing. But . . ." He bent his head and shaded his eyes with his hand.

Ashley didn't need for him to finish the sentence. She might not be a criminal investigator like Josiah had been, but she'd learned that the least likely person could be capable of the most despicable deed. He obviously knew that too.

"Did the lab find anything else?" Cole asked.

"He didn't say," Josiah answered. "The blood seems to be enough to make her a prime suspect."

"Wouldn't it be circumstantial?" Ashley asked. "Maybe she was there af—"

"She was definitely there," Josiah interrupted, his voice harsh. He stretched the fingers on both hands as if to force himself to relax. "I'm sorry. I didn't mean to snap. Rylee's always been naive. Innocent even. I can't imagine how she could be involved in something so awful." He swiped a hand over his face, then rested his chin in his palm.

"That's the question, isn't it?" Cole said. "Why would she? What's her connection with Oscar Moore?" He clapped Josiah's shoulder. "That's what we need to find out before suspecting her of anything. If she's innocent, she needs you on her side."

Josiah didn't speak for a long moment. Finally, he sat back in the chair. "I can't help suspecting her, much as I don't want to. But I'll never give up on her. Innocent or guilty, I'm not giving up on her."

As if sensing the depth of emotion in the room, Max sauntered to Ashley's chair and nudged her. She absentmindedly stroked his ear while her thoughts swirled. The blood on Rylee's shirt was important evidence, but was it enough to prove the young woman had killed Oscar Moore? If she had, what had she done with the knife? If it had been in the van, Wendy Heath would have found it when she did her inventory of the vehicle's contents.

Perhaps Rylee had thrown it out along the road somewhere between Oscar's place and where the accident had occurred. Which meant it could still be there.

The accident.

"Is anyone looking for the motorcyclist who ran Rylee off the road?" she asked.

Both Cole and Josiah shrugged. "What are you thinking?" Cole asked.

"That he's the murderer—or at least a valid suspect," Ashley said. She froze. Something gnawed at the edges of her mind, something she should know but couldn't remember.

Cole placed his hand on hers. "What's wrong?"

"Nothing." She flashed a smile. Hopefully whatever nagged at her would eventually come to mind. She stood to clear the table, but the entrance door buzzer sounded.

A feminine voice sounded from the front of the clinic. "Hello?

Anyone here?"

Not recognizing the newcomer, Ashley slipped on her lab coat as she walked toward the reception area. A woman who appeared to be in her midthirties stood inside the door. Large sunglasses sat atop auburn hair that had been pulled back into a stylish ponytail. Dressed in capris and a pretty blouse, she stood beside a rolling suitcase.

"You must be Dr. Hart," she said enthusiastically as she stepped forward. "I'm Savannah Drake."

Ashley held back her surprise as best she could. "Welcome to Aspen Falls. We weren't expecting you until tomorrow."

"That was the original plan," Savannah said. "But a business associate who pilots charter jets was flying to Denver, and he'd heard about my plight. He volunteered to drop me off in Vail, where I rented a car and, voilà! Here I am."

Coming from anyone else, the speech might have sounded pretentious, but Savannah delivered it with such ease she could have been discussing the weather.

"I'm glad you are," Ashley said. "Except we aren't ready for you. I mean, it is very nice to meet you, but the dogs are at their foster homes. Except for Ashes. He's resting in the back."

"Sweet little Ashes," Savannah crooned. "His mama is beside herself. But Ellen Hayes has been a wonder, keeping her updated and telling her not to worry."

"We wanted all the owners to know the dogs were in good hands," Ashley said, her mind racing with plans. It wouldn't take long to call each of the foster homes. The dogs could be brought to the clinic. But was there a rush? Ashley glanced at the rolling suitcase. Perhaps Savannah intended to spend the night in Aspen Falls.

"Are you driving back to Vail tonight?" Ashley asked.

Savannah shook her head, making her ponytail dance. "I'm not eager to drive those mountain roads in the dark. I am anxious to see my Bridey, though."

"Your beautiful spaniel is with a local family—one of our police officers, in fact. They've fallen in love with her, so you can be assured she's being spoiled rotten."

"I'm glad to hear it." Savannah's lips turned up into a mischievous grin. "As long as they're not *too* in love with her."

"I can call Wendy if you'd like, and tell her that you're here."

"I appreciate that, but I think I should get myself settled first. I'd love to see Ashes, though, if that's okay."

"Sure." Ashley led the way along the corridor. As they entered the large prep room, Savannah stopped to take in the space. Ashley paused beside her and imagined seeing the clinic through fresh eyes. Between the surgery rooms, the overnight and intensive care areas, and the clean, bright prep space, everything was in its right place.

"What a great space," Savannah gushed. "Everything is so shiny and new. I confess it's not what I expected to find in a historic fire station. I can't tell you how glad I am that our dogs ended up with you."

"The renovation wasn't very long ago," Ashley explained. She pointed to the corridor on the other side of the exam rooms, which stood in the center of the clinic's floor plan. "That hallway leads to radiology, the break room, the freezer room, and the lab. I'm very grateful Aspen Falls chose me to be their veterinarian."

"I can see why. From what I've seen so far, it's a charming town, and given the way you've all treated our dogs, it's full of good people. I hope to do a bit of exploring before heading home." Savannah had barely finished speaking when a clatter of toenails on the plank flooring sounded out an arrhythmic beat. Both Max and Cliffy rounded the corner from the break room, followed by Cole and Josiah.

Savannah beamed at the dogs, clearly charmed by their exuberance.

"Who are these handsome boys?"

"The Dalmatian is Max." At the sound of his name, Max joined Ashley, sitting close enough to lean into her leg. "The boxer is Cliffy." Ashley hesitated, not wanting to shock Savannah with the news of a local gruesome murder so soon after her arrival. "He's staying with me for a few days."

"And here, I thought she was asking about us." A flirtatious grin brightened Josiah's expression as he nudged Cole's arm.

As Ashley made introductions, Savannah tore her gaze from Cliffy, who stood between Josiah and Cole, to smile at the men. After that brief acknowledgment, she knelt on the floor. "His name is Cliffy?" Her quiet voice had a light tremor. She extended her hand, and Cliffy stepped toward her.

"According to his microchip information," Ashley said, puzzled by Savannah's actions. "He responds to that name."

"Hi, Cliffy." Savannah still spoke in a soft tone, but her voice held more confidence. "You sure are a handsome boy. The very handsomest boxer ever."

Cliffy stepped toward her, sniffed her fingers, then gently pushed against her. She wrapped her arms around him as tears flowed from her eyes. "You remember me, don't you? I can't believe it's you."

Ashley stared. How could this woman who had never been to Aspen Falls possibly know Cliffy?

11

Ashley stepped forward. “I don’t understand. Savannah, how do you know Cliffy?”

Savannah swiped her cheeks with the back of one hand as she kept the other around the dog. His demeanor was gentler than his interactions with Josiah, but his soft eyes were focused on Savannah. “He’s mine,” she said. “At least, he belongs to my family. He went missing several years ago from New Hampshire. How in the world did he get all the way out here?”

Nobody had an answer for her.

“How did you recognize him?” Josiah finally asked.

“My parents raise boxers. I was staying with them when he was born.” Savannah’s voice hitched but her eyes sparkled. “I guess you could say he was the runt of the litter. We weren’t sure he’d make it, but I couldn’t give up on him. A few days later, you’d never know he’d had any issues. My parents hadn’t planned to keep any of the puppies, but I begged them to hold on to Cliffy.”

Ashley perched on a stool she pulled from the doctor’s station. “How did he disappear?”

“It was a crazy time,” Savannah said. “Cliffy was about a year old and destined to be a champion of champions in conformation. Then my brother got sick. I don’t think Cliffy ever left his side. That is, until my brother left us.” She lowered her head, obviously doing her best not to cry. Ashley started to reach for a box of tissues, but Josiah got them first. He sat on the floor beside Savannah. Cliffy maneuvered the lower half of his body into Josiah's lap while keeping a front paw on Savannah's leg.

"I don't want to cry." Savannah dabbed at her eyes with a tissue. "I just can't believe he's really here."

"I'm sorry about your brother," Josiah said. "We all are."

Savannah took in Cliffy's sprawling length, then lifted her eyes to Josiah's. "You don't look like my brother. But there is something about you that's similar. I think Cliffy senses that."

"He does seem to like me," Josiah said, sounding a bit awkward.

Savannah smiled at him, then continued her story. "Cliffy went missing the day of the funeral. There were so many people coming through the house, so we thought he must have slipped out without anyone noticing. We searched and searched for him. But we didn't find him. And he didn't come home."

"New Hampshire is a long way from Colorado," Cole said, saying out loud what Ashley was thinking. "Someone must have picked him up, and then what? Moved west?"

"Cliffy probably knows the answer to that," Ashley said. "But I'm afraid he's not telling."

"It doesn't matter." Savannah hugged the boxer again. "Did you say you checked his microchip?"

"He was with the other dogs at the accident site," Ashley explained. "We checked the microchips on all of them."

Savannah frowned in confusion. "Then why didn't Ellen tell me about him?"

"You weren't listed as his owner," Ashley explained.

"But I must have been." The furrow between Savannah's eyebrows deepened. "Or maybe my mom or dad. They would have told me if anyone had called them, though."

Ashley let out a deep sigh. She didn't mistrust Savannah. In fact, she'd immediately liked her. The woman had the poise and attractiveness of a model, yet she sat on the floor in her expensive clothing with her legs crossed while Cliffy cuddled with her. The dog himself was providing proof that Savannah's story was true. He not only recognized her, but he also adored her the way a dog adored his owner.

But there was so much mystery surrounding Oscar's death and how Cliffy had ended up with Rylee and the show dogs. What if Savannah was part of some crazy plot instead of an innocent owner who had once lost her boxer?

"From what we know," Josiah said, "Cliffy belonged to someone named Oscar Moore."

"I don't know anyone by that name." Savannah arched an eyebrow. "Wait a minute. Why the past tense?"

"He died earlier this week. Someone killed him." Josiah bent his head and stroked Cliffy's ears. The dog's presence obviously brought him comfort. "The person who was driving the van full of dogs is my cousin. Right now, she's also the prime suspect for Oscar's murder."

"Your cousin?" Savannah eyed him with suspicion. "You mean she stole our dogs? Why would she do that?"

"I wish I knew." Josiah met Savannah's gaze.

Sensing how difficult it must be to admit Rylee's involvement in the dog theft, Ashley's heart went out to Josiah. Cole slipped his arm around her shoulders, and she nestled closer to him.

"Rylee was badly injured in the accident," Josiah went on evenly. "Earlier today, she regained consciousness, but it was for a few seconds, so she hasn't been able to tell us anything. I am sorry, and I am going to do everything I can to figure out what happened."

"What makes you think you can do that?" Savannah asked coolly.

Cole spoke up on behalf of his friend. "You can trust Josiah. We all want to know the truth."

Savannah lowered her eyes, her focus on Cliffy. He appeared determined to be as close as possible to both her and Josiah at the same time. "Cliffy trusts you," she said to Josiah. "If he hadn't been with a stranger for the past few years, that'd be enough for me. But now, I guess you're halfway there." She bent to kiss the boxer between his ears. "Tell me again about this man who had Cliffy."

"None of us really knew Oscar," Ashley said. "He wasn't one of my clients. When his name and address appeared on the microchip registry, Cole and I drove Cliffy out to his place. That's when we found him."

"*You* found him?" Savannah covered her mouth with her hand. "How awful."

"Actually, Cole found him," Ashley clarified. "Cliffy didn't want to go in the house, so I stayed outside with him."

"Why do the authorities believe your cousin killed him?" Savannah asked Josiah.

"The evidence is circumstantial." Josiah explained about the lab finding Oscar's blood on Rylee's clothes and about the phone call he'd received mere seconds before her accident. "I wish we could find who ran her off the road, but we don't have any leads."

"You don't believe she's guilty, do you?" Savannah asked.

"Of murder, no," Josiah said. "But I can't pretend she didn't steal the show dogs. I only wish I knew why."

"I'd like to know that too," Savannah murmured.

When she started to rise, Josiah gently lifted Cliffy from his lap, then stood and offered her a hand. She accepted his gesture and gracefully got to her feet despite Cliffy's efforts to crawl in her lap and keep her down on his level.

"It's getting late," Savannah said, "and I'm sure you've got better things to do than listen to my sad stories." When Ashley started to object, Savannah held up her hand. "You all have been very gracious and welcoming. I appreciate it. But it's time for me to be on my way."

"I'll call the Heaths and let them know you're here." Ashley reached for her phone.

Savannah glanced down at Cliffy, who lay at her feet. "I'm anxious to see Bridey, but once I do, I don't know if I'll be able to leave her again. If it's okay with you, I think I'd like to spend the evening getting reacquainted with Cliffy."

Ashley bit her lip, uncomfortable with what she had to say but knowing she had no other choice under the circumstances. "This may sound harsh, but I can't let you take Cliffy. Although he obviously likes you, he took to Josiah—a complete stranger—just as quickly. Chief Maloney let me bring him back here, but right now Cliffy is in a legal limbo."

"I understand your concern," Savannah said. "I'll tell you what. How about if we do a DNA test? You can match the results to my parents' records. I'll have Mom send a copy to you here at the clinic."

"That's a good start," Ashley said. "Where are you staying while you're in town?"

"I was hoping you could recommend a place. Apparently the local hotels are booked solid."

"What about the reservation you had for Rylee at the B&B?" Cole asked Josiah.

"I canceled it after the accident," Josiah said. "When I called earlier today to see about staying there myself, they'd already given it to someone else."

"I'm not surprised," Cole said. "Tourist season."

Ashley had a sudden flash of inspiration. "Why don't you stay with me? I have an extra bedroom, and that way you can be with Cliffy."

Savannah at first seemed startled by the invitation, but then a warm smile brightened her expression. "Are you sure you don't mind?"

"I'd love to have you," Ashley said warmly.

Savannah grinned. "Then I accept."

Ashley gestured toward the kennel room door. "We can head home after you see Ashes."

Josiah checked his watch. "I should be getting back to the hospital."

"Are you staying the night there again?" Cole asked. "I still have that couch, you know."

"I know." Josiah heaved a sigh. "Guess it depends on whether there's been any change."

Cole held out the key to his Nissan Rogue. "Take this. I can walk home."

"You're sure?" Josiah asked.

"Absolutely," Cole said. "If I don't see you tonight, I'll see you in the morning."

"Thanks, buddy." Josiah said his goodbyes and left.

Ashley escorted Savannah to the kennel room so she could spend a few moments with Ashes, then joined Cole in the break room. The two men had already cleared the table and taken out the trash.

"It was nice of you to invite Savannah to stay at your place." Cole took Ashley's hand and drew her close.

"Did you sense sparks between her and Josiah?" Ashley whispered so Savannah wouldn't accidentally overhear.

"Nah," Cole said, as he wrapped his arms around her. "Josiah is too worried about Rylee to think about romance."

Ashley wasn't so sure about that, but didn't feel the need to say so. She rested her head against Cole's shoulder and let his warmth ease all the anxieties she'd been feeling lately.

She prayed a similar peace for Josiah. And for the umpteenth time, she tried to convince herself Rylee had nothing to do with Oscar Moore's death.

12

Midmorning Friday, Ashley took advantage of a lull in the patient schedule to cross the expansive lobby of the renovated firehouse to get a pastry and her favorite specialty coffee from Mountain Goat Coffee Co. Melanie Lyons—whose husband, Aaron, worked with Cole—had moved her business into the location shortly after the renovation.

Ashley hoped that she'd be the sole customer, which would give her a chance to ask Melanie what she knew about Oscar Moore. After all, practically everyone in Aspen Falls frequented the coffee shop and either told Melanie all their news or talked loud enough to their friends that she couldn't help overhearing the conversations.

Not surprisingly for a tourist-season morning, however, the shop was bustling, keeping both college-age baristas at the counter busy. Ashley took her place in line, then noticed Savannah sitting at a nearby table—with Valerie Nelson.

The previous evening, Ashley and Savannah had changed into shorts and tees, gathered snacks and a pitcher of lemonade, and lounged on the back porch while Max and Cliffy chased each other. Savannah had been surprised to learn of Valerie's visit to the clinic and her demand to take the dogs.

"She didn't directly contact any of us," Savannah had told Ashley. She explained that Valerie had texted the handler who hired her about the theft of her vehicle with the dogs inside and he'd contacted the owners.

Their conversation had shifted to other topics with periods of companionable silence—silences when Savannah appeared deep in thought, her forehead wrinkled with tension and a brooding expression in her eyes.

Now she sat, posture perfect, in one of the café's wooden chairs, arms crossed, her eyes laser focused on the woman across from her.

Valerie bent forward and jabbed her finger onto the tabletop as if to punctuate whatever point she was making. Her eyes blazed, but she kept her voice low so only Savannah could hear her. However, she enunciated each word in such a way that it wasn't hard to read her lips.

It wasn't my fault!

Ashley experienced a moment of déjà vu. Rylee's whimpering cry, which had once again haunted Ashley's dreams, echoed inside her head. She closed her eyes until the moment passed. When she opened them again, Savannah and Valerie came back into focus.

Ashley was sure they were discussing the theft of the dogs, but Savannah didn't seem to be sympathetic to whatever explanation Valerie was trying to make. Though Valerie hadn't made a positive impression during her visit to the clinic, Ashley couldn't help feeling sorry for the young woman. Naturally Savannah was upset by what happened to the dogs, but it wasn't as if Valerie had purposely arranged for her vehicle to be stolen.

No one but Rylee knew the how and the why of the theft. According to a text Cole had sent Ashley earlier, Rylee had once again regained consciousness. She and Josiah had spoken for a moment before she drifted away again. He hadn't brought up the accident or the theft, though. As much as they all wanted to hear Rylee's side of the story, she needed to be stronger before broaching that topic.

As the thoughts coursed through Ashley's mind, Valerie suddenly noticed her in the line. The woman quickly stood, knocking her chair to the floor in the process. Savannah also rose and leaned across the table, drawing Valerie's attention back to her. In the stillness following the crash of the chair—which had halted all the other conversations in the coffee shop—Savannah's voice rang clear.

"Stay away from our dogs," she commanded. "And you'd better find another line of work because you'll never be a handler. I'll make sure of that."

Valerie retrieved her bag from where it had fallen on the floor and hurried to the door. She glared at Ashley on her way out of the shop.

Strange, Ashley mused. *Valerie acts as if she's almost as mad at me as she is at Savannah.* Didn't she understand that instead of making excuses—if that was, indeed, what she'd been doing—she should be apologizing and trying to make amends?

Granted, Ashley had to admit that Valerie may have reasons to be unhappy with her. Maybe she'd wanted to be the one to return the dogs to their owners to show that she was a responsible transporter, but Ashley had thwarted that effort. Valerie could also be upset because her vehicle had been stolen, then totaled in the accident. Thankfully, the dogs had survived with few injuries, but Valerie had the headache of repairing or replacing her vehicle. Maybe she was taking it out on anyone she could fix a glare on.

Shaking away thoughts of Valerie, Ashley focused on Savannah, who sat in her chair, elbows on the table and hands covering her face. Whether in embarrassment or because she was about to cry—maybe both—Ashley couldn't say for sure.

Crossing the café area, Ashley arrived at the table a moment after Melanie, who had come from behind the counter to investigate the commotion.

"Is everything okay?" Melanie asked as she righted the fallen chair.

Savannah barely nodded.

Ashley touched Savannah's shoulder. "Mind if I join you?"

Savannah didn't raise her head, but she gestured toward the empty chair. "Please." Her voice sounded tired and distraught. She took a deep breath, then raised her eyes to Melanie. "I'm sorry to cause a scene. It's not like me to do something like that. But this whole thing has me all out of sorts." She waved her hand in the air as if to encompass the events of the last couple of days in one motion.

"This is Savannah Drake," Ashley said to Melanie. "She owns one of the dogs that was found in the accident, and she's come to take all of them back to their owners. Savannah, this is my friend Melanie Lyons. She owns this coffee shop."

"Who was the woman who left in such a hurry?" Melanie asked after exchanging pleasantries. "She's been in here a couple of times recently, but she never says much, not even when there isn't a crowd like today."

"Her name is Valerie Nelson. She was supposed to take the dogs to Amarillo after a show in Colorado Springs," Ashley said, choosing her words carefully, not wanting to add to the gossip or say anything that might further upset Savannah. They'd clicked over their love of animals and sense of adventure, and Ashley wanted their friendship to continue.

Ashley had told Savannah about volunteering for World Vet Outreach the year after her graduation. She'd trained Ethiopian farmers to recognize the early symptoms of diseases in their livestock so they could receive effective treatment.

Savannah had shared her own yearlong volunteer experience for an overseas nongovernment organization that provided emergency disaster relief aid. Afterward, she'd gone to graduate school in Amarillo and stayed there. Because she owned her own specialty branding company, she also spent several weeks at a time at her parents' home, which was why she'd been in New Hampshire when Cliffy was born. Her parents had retired their kennel after their son's death, but they still had contact with others who raised champion boxers. Even so, when Savannah decided to return to the dog show world, she'd chosen a smaller breed because she lived in a condominium. After much research, she chose Cavalier King Charles spaniels for their sweet temperaments and affectionate natures.

"May I get you anything else?" Melanie asked Savannah as she cleared the table of Valerie's dishes.

"Thank you, but I'm fine," Savannah said.

"Have you ordered yet?" Melanie asked Ashley.

Ashley shook her head. "I just got here a few moments ago. But I can get back in line."

"Nonsense," Melanie said. "You stay here with Ms. Drake. Want your usual?"

Ashley beamed at her friend. "You're the best, Melanie. Thanks." Once Melanie had bustled off, Ashley sat in the seat vacated by Valerie and gave Savannah a compassionate look. "Do you want to talk about it?"

"She wanted me to release the dogs to her." Savannah rolled her eyes. "Can you believe it? I'm all for giving people second chances, but if we wanted to trust our dogs to her again, I wouldn't have flown here to get them myself."

"She seemed pretty angry when she left."

"Too angry." Savannah shivered. "I mean, I didn't expect her to grovel, but she could have at least said she was sorry. When I asked her if she'd locked her vehicle when she stopped at that rest area, she told me to read the police report. Was I wrong to ask? It's a simple question."

"Have you seen the police report?"

"Someone from the state police was supposed to email me a copy, but it hasn't shown up." Savannah twisted a napkin. "I am sorry for how stern I was with Valerie, but I'm not trusting her with those dogs."

"I don't trust her either, though I'm not sure why."

Savannah tilted her head and held her gaze steady. "One of the most important tools in my skill set is my ability to size people up. To see beyond the facade that they show the world and recognize what makes them tick. That's why I'm so good at helping entrepreneurs and creatives establish brands that work for them. That ability tells me that there's something off about Valerie Nelson." Savannah leaned forward. "Trust your instinct, Ashley. Believe me, it's your friend."

"Speaking of trust," Ashley said with an apologetic smile. "I need to ask you a question."

"You can ask me anything."

"I should have when you first arrived, but then you recognized Cliffy and it totally slipped my mind. It's about the dogs and their paperwork."

Savannah held up a hand. "Say no more." She pulled a folder from her bag. "I meant to give this to you when I arrived, but then I recognized Cliffy and—well, you know the rest." She grinned. "It's all in there. A notarized statement from each registered owner giving me full authority and responsibility for transporting the dogs from here to Amarillo. Plus paperwork proving ownership."

Ashley flipped through the pages. They were much more detailed and professional than the single page Valerie had been waving around. "Is it okay if I take these back to the clinic and make copies?"

"Those are yours to keep," Savannah said. "We each have a set of originals. All the owners signed two sets of documents."

"Thank you. I'm glad to have these."

Melanie arrived with a fresh cup of coffee for Savannah and Ashley's latte in a to-go cup. They chatted a few more minutes, then Ashley excused herself to return to the clinic. As she crossed the station lobby to the clinic, she noticed Valerie intently studying the hours posted on the front door of 3 Alarm Fur.

Was she waiting for Savannah to come out of the coffee shop so she could get into another argument with her? It was an argument that didn't make sense. Why was it so important to Valerie that she have possession of the dogs?

An icy finger trailed down Ashley's spine. Savannah was absolutely right. Something was off about Valerie Nelson.

13

Since Ellen had taken the day off to spend with her grandkids, Ashley was in charge of closing up the clinic. She finished with her final patient, escorted them out, and checked the clock. Seven minutes after three. Once again, she didn't have any farm calls after hours. As soon as she was done at work, she and Savannah planned to visit the dogs in their foster homes and then join the Talons Grip Adventure Team members for a much-needed practice.

Ashley plopped in the receptionist's chair and shut down the computer system while she waited for Savannah to return from her walk with Ashes. After leaving the coffee shop, Savannah had gone to Camp Paws, a local pet day care and store. Though the store didn't have a pet stroller for sale, Todd Bates, the owner, had one. He loaned it to Savannah so Ashes could go for a "walk" while resting his injured leg.

When the door opened, Ashley started to greet Savannah, but Katee Havenstar entered the clinic instead.

"This is a nice surprise." Ashley's enthusiastic greeting fell flat at the worried expression on Katee's face. "Is something wrong?"

"I hoped we could have a little chat." Katee glanced around. "Are we alone?"

"For now. But I am expecting someone any minute."

"Maybe I should come back later." Katee started to leave.

"No, please stay." Ashley rounded the desk and touched Katee's elbow. "The owner of one of the dogs found on that van arrived yesterday. She took the sheltie for a walk."

"In a dog stroller?"

Ashley couldn't help but smile. The tall auburn beauty would be noticed wherever she went. Add a dog stroller and she was unforgettable. "Yes."

"She went by the bookstore window going in the other direction as I was leaving," Katee said. "We should have a few minutes."

"Great." Ashley gestured toward the waiting area. "Please sit down and tell me what's troubling you." She sat in one of the empty chairs.

Katee perched on the edge of a seat, her fingers knotted in her lap. "First, I want to apologize for my strange behavior at the book club meeting the other night. Oscar's death was so unexpected. And then to learn that he'd been murdered." She shivered, then scooted back into the chair.

Ashley recalled how Katee had been afraid of not having an alibi for the time of the murder. "Chief Maloney doesn't suspect you, does he? What motive could you possibly have for killing Oscar Moore?"

"I guess that depends on what people choose to believe." Katee paused as if gathering her courage. "You see, I was probably the only person in Aspen Falls who knew his secret."

"His secret?"

"I've already told Chief Maloney all of this. With your knack for solving mysteries, and because you were there when his body was found, I think you should know too. After all, Oscar is dead now. I imagine it won't be long until all his fans learn the truth."

His secret? The truth? Ashley could barely hide her curiosity, and yet she sensed that the bookshop owner needed to tell the story in her own way and in her own time. She didn't want to rush Katee or make her feel more uncomfortable than she obviously already did.

"Have you ever read any books by Ansel Dodger?" Katee asked.

Surprised by the unexpected question, Ashley stared a moment before answering. "Once. Fantasy isn't one of my usual genres."

"Mine either. He's more of a storyteller than a wordsmith. But it's a popular genre, and he's managed to gain quite a large following."

"Including Oscar Moore," Ashley said.

For the first time since sitting down, Katee met Ashley's gaze. "You already know?"

"There was a copy of Ansel Dodger's latest book, *Tryst of Souls*, on the back patio at Oscar's house," Ashley explained. "I saw it when I was out there with Cliffy. It was strange to me because I didn't think that book had been released yet. I guess Oscar must have known the right people."

"He didn't know the right people. He *was* the right people." Katee bit her lip. "Oscar was Ansel Dodger."

"Oh." Ashley sat back as she processed that information. The surprising news ignited a sudden insight. "That's why you had autographed copies. He trusted you with his secret."

"He did. Until a couple of weeks ago."

"What happened?"

"He accused me of posting his manuscript drafts online. As if I'd ever do anything like that."

"I don't understand," Ashley said. "How would you have access to any of his drafts?"

"I go out there sometimes to pick up vegetables or to deliver books. He was a bit of a recluse, and he certainly didn't want anyone to know of his secret author life. Frankly, he was over-the-top paranoid. But he trusted me." Katee took a breath. "I'd order books he wanted for research under my name and take them out to him when they arrived. That kept third-party deliveries to a minimum. He really didn't like too many people coming to his home."

"That doesn't explain how you'd get his manuscript drafts," Ashley said. "Weren't they on his laptop?"

"He used a laptop, of course. But he liked to print out chapters and read them on paper. I'd read through them sometimes to give him feedback. Then he'd pile them, draft after draft, on top of each other in a box that he kept in a back bedroom." Katee shifted uneasily. "He realized several chapters from his latest manuscript were missing and then discovered they'd been posted on a fan site. He was absolutely livid, shouting and flailing his arms around."

"Oh no," Ashley murmured.

Katee's shoulders sank, and tears welled in her eyes. "He said I was the only one who could have taken them. But I didn't, Ashley. I didn't even know about the boxes. And I didn't kill him either, but I was out there early in the morning, and I don't have an alibi for later. If we don't find out who really killed him, I might be blamed."

Ashley struggled to process all this new information. "What did Chief Maloney say when you talked to him?"

"Not to leave town." Katee's weak smile tugged at Ashley's heart, and Ashley placed a comforting hand on her friend's arm. "I don't think he believes I'm guilty, but he has to pursue every lead. I guess I'm a person of interest."

"Why don't you have an alibi?" The bookstore would have been open when Oscar was killed. "Weren't you working?"

"I opened late that day." Katee's tears slid down her cheek. "It was the fifth anniversary of my dad's death."

"I'm so sorry."

Katee gave a wan smile of appreciation for the sympathy. "It's always a hard day. But there's something about it being the fifth anniversary that made it extra hard. After I left Oscar's place, I drove to Dad's favorite fishing spot up near Aspen Glade. We went there so often as a family.

It's very secluded and peaceful. As I sat there, I could almost believe Dad was with me, casting his line and slowly reeling it back in again."

"That must have been comforting for you."

"It was," Katee agreed. "But I have no proof of where I was. I didn't see anyone up there, and it wouldn't matter if I had. The route up to that mountain is a couple of miles from Oscar's house. Even if I hadn't stopped to see him, it wouldn't have been out of my way to do so." She dug a tissue from her bag and dabbed at her tears. "You believe me, don't you?"

"I absolutely do," Ashley reassured her. "I'm still trying to wrap my mind around a famous author living in anonymity a few miles from here. Do you know why he kept his career such a secret?"

"He said once that his joy was in the imagining of strange stories. That he wasn't interested in the trappings of fame or how fickle it could be. He apparently started out when indie publishing, which is what he used, became a more respectable alternative to traditional publishing. As his fan base grew, he became even more guarded about protecting his identity."

"I'm surprised no one found it out," Ashley said. "I didn't think it was possible to keep such a secret in the Internet age."

"Somehow he managed it." Katee stood and threw away the tissue. "I need to get back. I told Brandy I wouldn't be gone very long and that I'd bring her back an iced coffee." Brandy Harding, the mayor's daughter, attended college in Boulder and worked part-time at Bookaroo during her summer breaks.

"I'm here anytime," Ashley said. "If there's anything I can do or that you need, please let me know."

"There's one thing," Katee said, "though I feel like a horrible person for asking."

"What is it?"

"I heard through the grapevine that Chief Maloney has another suspect. The young woman who wrecked her van."

"Yes, Rylee Goodwin. She's regained consciousness a couple of times, but not long enough to be questioned."

"She was at Oscar's place?"

"It appears so." Ashley pressed her lips together, unsure of how much she was at liberty to tell Katee. As much as she wanted to reassure her friend, she didn't want to throw more suspicion on Rylee. "As far as I know, though, no one has found any connection between her and Oscar Moore or any reason why she would have been there."

"I almost envy her." Katee gave a wry laugh. "She's not aware that she's a murder suspect. I'm so afraid of what will happen if she's innocent and the chief's full attention shifts to me." She shook her head. "But it would be awful to hope she was guilty."

"Honestly, I don't believe either you or Rylee had anything to do with Oscar's death. I'm sure Chief Maloney will find the murderer. Or maybe Josiah will. He doesn't believe Rylee could have done it either."

"You mean Josiah Hunter?"

Ashley nodded. After the EMTs removed Rylee from the van, Josiah had managed to snag her laptop and phone. The police hadn't secured a warrant for them yet, and he wasn't about to hand them over freely before doing his own search. During his long hours at the hospital, he had been scouring her browsing history and phone records. So far, he'd found nothing.

"He's such a nice young man. I heard they are related." Katee patted Ashley's arm and stood. "My money is on you solving the mystery. Like I said, you have a knack for uncovering the truth."

Ashley gave a self-deprecating chuckle. "Not this time. I'm more than happy to leave the sleuthing to the professionals." She meant what she said—she'd been involved in enough frightening situations and would be happy to live out the rest of her days without experiencing any more. And yet, she felt sorry for Katee. The woman shouldn't be under a cloud of suspicion simply because she'd chosen to honor her father's memory with a personal trip to one of his favorite places.

Though she couldn't be as sure of Rylee's innocence, Ashley trusted Josiah's instincts. He was naturally biased to believe his cousin to be innocent, but he was doing his best to view the case in a dispassionate manner. The young woman was a naive idealist—that was clear from the stories Josiah had shared with Ashley and Cole about her. He'd also told stories of how she fainted at the sight of blood and never watched violent movies. He insisted her aversion to gore made it highly unlikely she'd attacked Oscar, considering the method used.

If only someone could locate the motorcyclist who'd run Rylee off the road. As each day passed, finding that person became less likely. Their best hope was for Rylee to regain consciousness and enough stability to give her side of the story.

As Katee prepared to leave the clinic, the door opened. Savannah entered carrying Ashes in her arms and pulling the stroller behind her.

"Is he okay?" Ashley said, immediately concerned.

"As long as being spoiled isn't a disease, he's grand," Savannah replied with a good-natured chuckle. "We've had the best time. I think I'm falling in love with Aspen Falls."

"That's music to my ears," Katee said. "I saw you walk past the bookstore earlier."

Ashley introduced the two women as Savannah gently placed Ashes on the floor. The sheltie lay down so his back legs sprawled out behind him.

"He must be feeling better," Ashley said. "The fresh air was good for him."

"For me too." Savannah tilted her head. "I have a feeling I interrupted something. If I did, I'm sorry. Should I go for an ice cream run?"

"No need. I was on my way out," Katee said. "How long will you be in town?"

"Depends on my pilot," Savannah explained. "I hitched a ride from Amarillo with a friend who owns an air charter service. He dropped me off in Vail before going on to Denver. We were supposed to go back to Amarillo tomorrow, but while I was out exploring the town, he sent me a text. Something has come up, and he needs to stay in Denver a couple more days. Guess I'll be driving home instead of flying."

"Or you can stay with me a while longer," Ashley suggested. "That is, if you want to, and the other owners don't mind."

"I was actually hoping you'd say that," Savannah said. "I talked to my attorney earlier about how to reclaim Cliffy. I don't suppose you've heard anything about who the executor of Oscar Moore's estate might be."

"I haven't." Ashley glanced at Katee. As one of the few people who knew of Mr. Moore's double life, it wasn't improbable to think she might know the details of his estate planning. Ashley couldn't ask her outright in front of Savannah, since she didn't want to break any confidences.

"What do you mean by 'reclaim Cliffy'?" Katee asked. "You mean Oscar's dog?"

"He's my dog." Savannah explained how the boxer had gone missing from her parents' New England home and how surprised she'd been to find him when she arrived at the clinic. "Ashley did a DNA swab, and we're waiting for the results to compare them with my family's records. But I know it's him."

Katee's eyes lit up with amazement. "That's incredible."

"Katee, did Oscar ever tell you how he got Cliffy?" Ashley asked.

"It'd be great if we could trace Cliffy's journey from New Hampshire to Colorado."

"I'm curious about that too," Savannah said. "I tried to find Oscar online, but I gave up after scouring the first ten pages. It's too common a name, and none of the results were for someone from around here."

"You'd have never found anything," Katee said. She took a deep breath. "I was just telling Ashley that Oscar was a novelist who wrote under the pen name Ansel Dodger. He guarded his privacy to the point of paranoia. Even his author's social media presence was driven by his fans and a made-up publicist."

"A what?" Ashley asked.

Katee chuckled at Ashley's response. "He made up a publicist who sent out press releases and marketing materials whenever a new book released. But it was all Oscar."

"A man of many faces," Savannah said. "I sure would like to see one of those faces."

"Chief Maloney has a copy of his driver's license." Ashley's expression brightened. "And I think I know someone else who might have a photo. Josiah Hunter is doing his own investigation so he can clear his cousin."

"I'll give Josiah a call." Savannah pulled her phone from her back pocket and gestured toward the hallway. "Do you mind if I step away for a little privacy?"

"Not at all," Ashley said.

Savannah bent to pick up Ashes. "Come on, boy. I bet you can use a drink of water." As she headed toward the break room, the sheltie under one arm and her phone in her other hand, her voice drifted back to the waiting area. "Hi, Josiah. It's me, Savannah."

Ashley and Katee exchanged an amused glance. "I had no idea she had Josiah's phone number," Ashley said.

"Perhaps he's the primary reason she's falling in love with Aspen Falls," Katee said with a smile. Her mood seemed much lighter than it had been when she'd first arrived at the clinic. "Now, I really must be going or Brandy will think I'm never coming back. Guess I need to get her a pastry along with that iced coffee I promised."

Ashley chuckled, then locked the front door behind Katee. She didn't want to interrupt Savannah if she was still on the phone with Josiah, but the time was quickly passing by. They still needed to visit the foster homes before meeting up with Talons Grip for practice.

As she tidied the waiting area, Ashley reviewed all that Katee had told her about Oscar's private life. After confronting Katee, had Oscar discovered who had actually stolen the manuscript pages? Had he confronted that person too?

If he was murdered because of his secret, then that narrowed the pool of suspects to a few. And hopefully the refined list didn't include Rylee Goodwin.

14

Once Ashes was settled again in his kennel, Ashley and Savannah left the clinic to visit the foster families. Savannah was impressed with the loving care that Rugby, the papillon, and the three Brussels griffons were receiving and enjoyed her time with their temporary caretakers. All the families assured Savannah that they were happy to keep the dogs as long as they needed a place to stay.

At Savannah's request, Ashley saved the Heath home for last. Wendy, dressed in a casual sundress and flip-flops, opened the door to them. Though they attended the same church and a few other activities, Ashley still found it strange whenever she encountered Wendy dressed in something other than her police uniform. Without the bulkiness of her utility belt, gun and holster, and shoulder microphone, she appeared even more petite and athletic.

Ashley made introductions, and Savannah thanked Wendy for providing Bridey with a temporary home.

"It's been a pleasure," Wendy said. "She's a lovely dog. My daughter, Andie, is out back with her. This way."

She escorted them from the foyer to the rear patio. When Savannah stepped through the sliding glass door, Bridey gave a sharp bark and flung herself into her owner's open arms. She licked every part of Savannah that she could reach, whimpering and wiggling all over. Savannah gathered the red-and-white spaniel to her chest and buried her face in the soft fur. The other dogs had clearly been happy to see Savannah, but none of them had greeted her so exuberantly.

"It's been so hard not seeing you," Savannah murmured. "But you look happy as can be. What a good girl you are."

"We gave her this." Andie, a sophomore at the local high school, held out a stuffed hedgehog. The smile the teen gave Savannah was a little sad. "Is it okay if she keeps it to remember us by? It's her favorite."

"I can see why." Savannah shifted Bridey to one arm and took the toy. "She has one like it at home. How sweet of you to get this for her."

Andie's eyes brightened. "Does she really? I got her a miniature tennis ball too, but she doesn't pay much attention to it. And I've brushed her every day."

Savannah laughed. "That's more than I do. Thank you for taking such good care of her." As if to also express her thanks, Bridey wiggled out of Savannah's arms and scurried to Andie, received a belly rub, then raced back to Savannah.

"Mom told me that you raise show dogs," the teen said. "I think I may want to do that someday. Do you have any advice?"

While Savannah and Andie talked, Ashley drew Wendy aside. "Is there any news about Mr. Moore's murder?" she asked. "Anything you're allowed to say, I mean."

"I wish I had something to tell you." The space between Wendy's eyes narrowed. "There seems to be quite a bit of mystery about Oscar Moore."

"Katee told me he wrote novels under a pseudonym."

"Or perhaps he wrote novels as himself and lived life as a pseudonym," Wendy said quietly, almost as if she were talking to herself rather than Ashley.

"What do you mean?" Ashley asked.

"Nothing, really." Wendy gazed into the distance as if focusing on something that Ashley couldn't see. "Let's just say that learning about Oscar's literary career has opened up a whole new line of investigation."

"Does that mean Rylee is no longer a suspect?"

"I didn't say that," Wendy said. "Rylee's fingerprints were found at the murder scene."

"You took her fingerprints while she was unconscious?" Ashley was aghast at the notion and surprised that Josiah hadn't mentioned it. "Wouldn't you need a court order to do something like that?"

"We didn't have to take her prints," Wendy said. "Rylee Goodwin is already in the system."

Of course she would be. Josiah had mentioned she'd been arrested because of her idealistic activism.

"I wish she'd regain consciousness so we could question her." Wendy's lips curved into an apologetic smile. "I didn't mean it like that. Sometimes I'm too much of a cop."

"I understand," Ashley reassured her. "I pray for her to get better every day, but I'm also eager to hear her side of the story. And I wish the mysterious motorcyclist would come forward."

"You'll be waiting a long time for that to happen." Wendy took Ashley's arm and tugged her farther away from Savannah and Andie. "Are you sure such an individual even exists?"

"Are you saying she had the accident on purpose?" That didn't make any sense. Why would Rylee go to all the trouble of stealing the dogs only to risk killing herself?

"Not on purpose. But perhaps the accident didn't happen the way we think it did."

The doubt in Wendy's tone sucked the air from Ashley's lungs. She had never considered the idea that Rylee might have been lying when she called Josiah. It took no more than a second of consideration for her to dismiss that idea now.

"I heard her," Ashley said, more forcefully than she intended. But Wendy had to know the call was real. Rylee's fear had been real. "Josiah was standing almost as close to me as you are now. Rylee was terrified to her core, in a way no one could fake. I've had nightmares about that call." Ashley searched Wendy's face, seeking confirmation that she believed her.

But even though Wendy wasn't wearing her uniform, she'd transformed into Officer Heath at that moment. Her impassive expression didn't reveal any of her thoughts.

"If you'd heard her—if you'd seen how shaken Josiah was when Rylee screamed—you'd know she was telling the truth. Besides, no one could have made up such a tall tale if they'd simply lost control of their vehicle. They wouldn't have time." Ashley's facial muscles tensed as her conviction grew in the face of Wendy's questioning. "Someone hit her vehicle. It sounded like someone shot at her. I know that accident was real as surely as if I'd seen it."

Wendy's gaze didn't waver for several long seconds. Then her expression softened, and she touched Ashley's arm. "I believe you. I believe Rylee."

The breath that Ashley hadn't realized she was holding whooshed from her lungs, leaving her relieved and drained. She didn't know why she needed to defend Rylee—a young woman she didn't know and had never even laid eyes on except for brief glimpses at the accident scene—but the rightness of that need increased her belief in Rylee's innocence when it came to Oscar Moore's murder.

As Wendy returned to Andie and Savannah, Ashley relived Rylee's frightened plea for help.

He's trying to kill me.

Somewhere, a stranger on a motorcycle held the key to unlocking this mystery.

That person, not Rylee, must have killed Oscar Moore.

After leaving the Heath home, where Savannah had generously—though with a catch in her throat—allowed Andie to keep Bridey another night, Ashley drove to the medical center to meet up with Cole and Josiah.

From there, they piled into Cole's Nissan Rogue and headed to the river landing. During the drive, Josiah updated them on Rylee's condition. She'd awakened long enough to ask about the dogs. Josiah had to reassure her several times that they were all safe and unharmed. He intentionally hadn't mentioned the injuries that Ashes and Rugby had received because he didn't want to upset her. When he asked about the accident, however, she claimed she couldn't remember what had happened, nor did she seem to remember being on the phone with him at the time.

Concerned for her emotional well-being, Josiah didn't ask about the motorcyclist or Oscar Moore. A few moments later, she'd drifted into another deep sleep. He'd almost skipped out on the race practice in case she awoke again, but the matronly nurse who acted as Rylee's primary caregiver had encouraged him to go. During a brief aside when Josiah and Savannah stopped at a vending machine for a snack, Cole confided to Ashley his belief that Chief Maloney wanted Josiah out of the room when Rylee awakened again so he or Deputy Chief Jana Lewis could talk to her in private.

As they wound their way along the mountain road, Josiah's somber mood gradually improved until he was laughing and joking with the rest of them. Ashley credited Savannah's quick wit and gentle humor for transforming him back into the easygoing, personable guy Ashley had known before Rylee's accident. A tinge of worry still clouded his expression, but he obviously wanted to make a good impression on the Texan beauty sharing the back seat with him.

When they arrived at their destination, Rob and Lorie Tavish were already unloading three orange kayaks into the Eagle River. Ashley scooted from the Nissan and filled her lungs with the sun-warmed mountain air.

The broad river, which they'd crossed once on their drive, snaked between rocky banks. An S curve slowed the river's speed at the landing, which made it a popular place for launching watercraft. However, between the landing and the team's destination, the river churned between jutting rocks as its width narrowed. Navigating these rapids was the most challenging part of the trip.

"Here's the plan," Rob said as Cole, Josiah, and Lorie gathered around him. "The three of you line up right about there." He gestured toward a patch of weeds not far from the sandbar. "The time starts when I say go. You race to the kayaks and get them in the river. I'll stay here until you're on your way."

He placed a map on the hood of the Nissan and pointed out locations along the river as he talked. "We're here, and this is the destination. I'll take the trailer there." He indicated another spot about halfway between the landing and the destination. "This is our checkpoint. Ashley, you and Savannah need to drive there as soon as the kayaks are in the water. Once all three kayaks have passed that point, join me at the destination. If any of you gets in trouble, let us know." He handed out portable radios. The ones for the kayaks were in waterproof bags. "Any questions?"

"I don't suppose there's room for a fourth member of the team, is there?" Savannah smiled. "I haven't been on the water in ages."

"You kayak?" Josiah asked.

"I was on a crew team in college," Savannah answered.

"You're full of surprises, aren't you?"

"A woman of mystery and many hidden talents. That's me."

"I'll keep that in mind."

Rob held up a stopwatch. "If you're all done with the flirtatious banter, I'd like to get started."

"Who's flirting?" Savannah exclaimed.

"There's no banter," Josiah insisted at the same time.

Cole lightly punched Josiah's arm. "You're protesting too much. Let's do this thing."

Giving over to the teasing, Savannah wiggled her fingers at Josiah and batted her eyelashes. "See you at the finish line, *dahling*," she said in an exaggerated accent.

Josiah blushed but grinned. "Counting the minutes," he said, tossing the words over his shoulder as he joined Cole and Lorie at the imaginary start line Rob had indicated earlier.

The three racers strapped on helmets, then focused on the kayaks lined up end to end on the sandbar. Rob positioned himself where they could see him and the kayaks, but he wasn't in their way. He raised one hand in the air and held the stopwatch with the other.

"On your mark," Rob called. "Get set. Go!" At the last command, he lowered his hand and clicked the stopwatch.

The racers hurried to the kayaks. Lorie grabbed a paddle while Cole and Josiah overturned the first one and set it in the water. The instant Lorie settled in the seat, they pushed her toward the current. She immediately maneuvered downstream.

The men briskly flipped the second and third kayaks. Using the paddles to push away from the sandbar, they soon trailed Lorie.

"You head out first, Ashley," Rob said as he handed her the map. "I want you to be at the checkpoint before they pass by. You won't have to speed or anything, but don't dawdle."

"We're on our way." Ashley and Savannah climbed into Cole's Nissan and headed toward the checkpoint.

"I'll be your navigator," Savannah said, taking the map. "I've never done anything quite like this, but I participated in a three-day survival camp once. We had to find our way across an island with a compass and a hand-drawn sketch."

"How did you do?" Ashley asked as she drove away from the landing's makeshift parking area.

"My partner and I finished first." Though she didn't sound boastful, Savannah's tone held a hint of mirth.

"Sounds like there's more to the story."

Savannah chuckled. "There is. To be honest, we had a bit of luck soon after we started. My partner—we'd been best friends forever—was reading the map upside down, so we were going totally in the wrong direction." She paused to study the map in her hands. "Take the next right and follow the road to a T-intersection."

"Got it." Ashley slowed. "How did you finish first if your partner was reading the map wrong?"

"We found a couple of old fishermen who took pity on us. They could tell from the sketch where we were supposed to end up, so they drew a shortcut for us and took us to the right trail. I studied that map until I had it memorized. We were the first team to arrive."

Ashley opened her mouth to say something, but Savannah held up a finger.

"Now, I know what you're thinking," she went on. "'Isn't that cheating?' Of course it is. But since we were only there to meet guys—did I mention I was still in college at the time?—we confessed the secret to our success and were immediately disqualified. As they say, all's well that ends well. The real winners were handsome hunks who took us out to dinner for a consolation prize. We were the perfect foursome. For a while." Her tone became wistful, then she pointed through the windshield. "There's the T. Left here."

"I see it." Ashley braked, glancing at Savannah before making the turn. "Is it okay if I ask what happened to the foursome?"

"My friend and her guy celebrated their tenth anniversary last month. My guy and I came about this close to getting engaged." She held her finger and thumb less than an inch apart from one another. "But then I got an opportunity to work with the NGO and he was accepted into a doctoral program, which meant three more years of school. So we said our goodbyes and promised to stay in touch." She shrugged and waved her hand. "We didn't keep that promise."

"Any regrets?" Ashley kept her tone light so the question didn't seem too much like prying. The sparks between Savannah and Josiah couldn't be more obvious, but if Savannah still carried a torch for an old flame, Ashley wanted to know about it—even if it wouldn't be her place to tell Josiah. *Please say no.*

"None at all," Savannah said as she traced a fingertip along the map. "You'll be making another left, but not until after we pass what I think is a pond on our right." She shifted her attention to the landscape. "I saw him again at the anniversary party because of course he was the best man and I was the maid of honor. I met his wife, who is a saint, and his kids, who are all adorable, and we all laughed and had the best of times. So, no. No regrets." She sighed contentedly then fixed her gaze on Ashley. "What about you? Any handsome hunks in your past?"

Though Ashley focused on navigating the curves, she could see Savannah's insistent stare in her peripheral vision.

"There was a guy once," she admitted. "Same song as yours, just a different verse."

"But now you have Cole."

Heat burned Ashley's cheeks. Though they'd been dating a while, the romance still felt new and fragile. Except not exactly *fragile.* Their relationship, from the beginning, had a strength born of mutual respect, compatibility, and affection. Sometimes it felt as if she'd known Cole all of her life. Or, perhaps to be more precise, she'd known the idea of him all her life. It had taken almost forty years for their paths to cross.

"Yes." She smiled broadly. "I have Cole. And there's the pond." She signaled to make the left turn though they were the only car on the rural road.

"This road takes us to the river, then curves so we run parallel to it for a couple of miles." Savannah studied the map again. "The checkpoint is behind a gas station on the left."

After they parked, the two women followed a dirt path leading to a bluff overlooking the river. Wooden picnic tables and grills were scattered beneath the tall pines. A boardwalk and steep stairs led from the plateau to a long sandbar occupied by a young couple, their gangly dog, and a canoe.

Once again, Ashley and Savannah fell into a companionable conversation, as if they were old friends who hadn't seen each other in ages but could pick up where they left off no matter how long they were apart. They laughed at the antics of the dog—Ashley pegged him as a retriever mix less than a year old—who was trying to catch one of the fish darting in the shallows. He splashed the water with his paw, then submerged his nose beneath the surface.

A movement upriver caught Ashley's attention, and she stood on the bench of the picnic table to get a better view. "I think they're coming."

Savannah went to the edge of the bluff. "Yep. All three of them."

Ashley joined her and shaded her eyes against the sun. Since the trio were wearing identical helmets, it was practically impossible to tell who was in which kayak. However, it looked like—yes, she was sure of it—Cole was in the lead with the other two close on his tail.

She and Savannah whooped and hollered like two teenagers at a music concert to get their attention. The kayakers raised their paddles in salute as they passed by, then immediately resumed the business of paddling.

Ashley used the portable radio to contact Rob. "They just passed the checkpoint. All's well."

"Great," he said. "See you here soon."

On the walk back to the Nissan, Ashley reveled in the respite the time with her friends, both old and new, had given her. For a while she'd been able to put the mystery of who'd killed Oscar Moore out of her mind. Yet it lingered, an unwelcome and pesky guest, on the fringes of her thoughts. She knew she'd soon have to face the mystery again in her quest to help prove Rylee's innocence.

15

Cole flipped burgers on Ashley's backyard grill while she prepared the veggies for a fresh garden salad. Savannah pulled condiments from the refrigerator and arranged them on a tray with plates, napkins, and a flatware caddy. Josiah threw balls for Max and Cliffy to chase while chatting on his cell phone.

"Thanks again for inviting us over," Savannah said to Ashley. "It's too bad that Lorie and Rob couldn't come."

"I wish they had, but reservations at Canyon Farm Bistro can be hard to come by in tourist season, so I don't blame them for passing." Ashley added a layer of sliced cucumbers to the large salad bowl. "At least Josiah said yes. I wasn't sure he would."

"After he checked on Rylee. He's obviously very devoted to her." A smile lit up Savannah's face. "I like a man who cares about his family."

"It's an important quality." Ashley completely agreed with her—she appreciated Cole's close relationship with his family too—but she couldn't help but be amused by Savannah's eagerness to talk about Josiah. The spark seemed to have flared into a flame.

Ashley rummaged through a drawer for salad tongs and placed them in the bowl. She set the bowl next to a platter of sliced tomatoes, onions, and cheese. "The salad's ready. Did you get the dressing?"

"Ranch and Italian." Savannah pointed to the bottles on her tray. "Anything else?"

Ashley scanned the tray, which—in addition to the typical condiments of mustard, ketchup, and mayo—included two jars of different kinds of pickles. Everything needed for a customized burger. "Can you carry all that?"

Savannah grinned. "Watch me."

Ashley juggled the platter and salad bowl while Savannah carried the tray. As they joined Cole on the patio, Josiah finished his phone call. Cole gave thanks for the food and the fellowship, then everyone added toppings to their burgers and helped themselves to the salad.

On the way back to town, the men had told Ashley and Savannah about their kayaking experience and how Lorie had managed to maneuver through a series of large boulders to take a huge lead. Cole beat Josiah by only a few seconds, but Rob had been impressed by all their times. He expected the team to do well in the competition and especially wanted Talons Grip to beat the Fighting Fit racers. Lorie wanted that too, since Dina Ford, her business partner and the other co-owner of Summit Fitness, captained the opposing team. Bragging rights were at stake as well as a couple of friendly wagers involving who had to clean the fitness center locker rooms.

Josiah took a long swallow of iced tea. "That call was from a computer whiz I worked with from time to time when I was still in the military. A couple of days ago, I asked him to find everything he could on Oscar Moore."

"Did he find anything interesting?" Cole asked.

"That'd be a yes." Josiah speared a cucumber and swiped it through a pool of Italian dressing. "Oscar Moore moved to this area a few years ago. That's when he bought his place and got a Colorado driver's license. He paid property taxes and appears to have been a model citizen of the Centennial State."

"Did he already have Cliffy?" Savannah asked.

At the sound of his name, the boxer sauntered toward the table and placed his round muzzle on the bench seat between Josiah and Savannah.

Ashley noticed that they both reached down to pat Cliffy's head at the same time. Their hands must have touched under the table because Savannah's cheeks suddenly grew pink and Josiah almost choked on his cucumber.

Ashley exchanged a smile with Cole. *Were we ever like that?* Surely they must have been, since she remembered their friends exchanging similar glances at times. Cole took her hand and gave it a squeeze. She squeezed back, then returned her hand to her burger before a tomato slice could slip out of her bun.

"I don't know the answer to that, but it should be easy to find out," Josiah replied. "I'll check animal control to see when he got a license. That is, *if* he got a license."

"Where did he live before?" Cole asked.

"Not a clue. My pal can find no trace of an Oscar Moore, at least not this particular Oscar Moore, before he came to Colorado."

"You're saying Oscar Moore isn't his real name?" Ashley asked. "What about his pseudonym? Wendy suggested that could be his real name and 'Oscar Moore' is a fake."

Cole stared at her in surprise. "What pseudonym?"

Ashley grimaced. "I forgot you didn't know. Katee told me in confidence." Her voice faltered. "She also told Savannah, so I'm not sure it's a secret anymore. But if it is . . ."

"My pal found out all about that too." Josiah addressed Cole. "Oscar Moore wrote fantasy novels under the name Ansel Dodger. Part of his shtick was to never have his photograph taken, never to do book signings, and never meet with fans. Guess we know now that it wasn't so much a shtick as a necessity. Our buddy Oscar was in hiding, and he didn't want anyone to find him."

Cole grunted in disbelief. "Ansel Dodger was actually Oscar Moore? I can't believe it. I've read a couple of his books. Even talked to Oscar once about one of them. He never let on."

"He didn't dare," Josiah said, "especially not if he was in hiding. Anyway, to get back to Ashley's question, the pseudonym is a pseudonym. Then again, Oscar Moore is a fake name too."

"So who was he really?" Savannah bent her head to gaze at Cliffy. "And how did he get my dog?"

"My pal is still digging," Josiah replied. "His next step is to acquire Oscar's driver's license photo and run it through a facial recognition program. That could take some time."

"'Acquire?'" Cole snorted. "Is that a synonym for 'illegally obtain'?"

"Perhaps," Josiah admitted. "As I told Savannah yesterday, I don't have the photo. Fortunately, my pal has his own means and methods. I don't question them."

"But won't the crime lab do that?" Ashley asked.

"Depends on how important it is to find out Moore's true identity to solve his murder," Josiah said. "They don't have unlimited resources. My professional guess is that they'll wait until all the other evidence is processed before taking that step. If they don't have to, they won't."

"I wish I could see his driver's license." Savannah's tone bordered on irritable, though Ashley couldn't blame her. She'd be upset too if she found Max living with a stranger after he'd been missing for such a long time.

"I wish I had it for you," Josiah said.

"I just remembered something," Ashley announced, rising from her seat. "Why didn't I think of this earlier? Mr. Moore's photo was in *The Avalanche News*. It's in the recycling bin in the garage. I can get it for you."

"Hold on a sec, Ashley." Josiah asked as he pulled out his phone and opened an Internet app. "Does the paper have a website?"

"Mostly for classified ads," Cole replied, "but a story as big as this should be on the landing page."

"I've got it." Josiah tapped on a photo to enlarge it and held out his phone so Savannah could see the screen.

Her eyes rounded as she stared at the photo. "It can't be. I don't believe it."

Josiah's brows furrowed as he focused on Savannah. All the color had left her face and her hands covered her mouth. "Don't tell me you know him."

When Savannah finally spoke, her voice caught in her throat, coming out strained and soft. "I do know him."

"How?" Josiah asked.

"He belonged to the same dog club as my parents. In New Hampshire." Tears welled in her eyes as she bent to wrap her arms around Cliffy. In that contorted position, she was only partially visible from Ashley and Cole's side of the table. "Cliffy didn't go missing. That man stole him."

16

The story came out in fits and starts, with Josiah fumbling to type notes on his phone until Ashley brought him a pen and notepad. The man they'd known as Oscar Moore was known to Savannah as Ogden Sadler. As a professional dog handler, he'd successfully shown three or four of the Drake family's boxers until they received their championships.

When movie trailers appeared for a kids' movie featuring a smart and endearing Keeshond, Oscar had tossed his professional ethics aside to capitalize on the looming demand for the breed. Unsurprisingly, Oscar was right about the breed's sudden though brief popularity, but what appalled the other members of the club was his total lack of regard for purposeful breeding practices. Before long, Oscar appeared to be operating a puppy mill instead of a respectable kennel.

Eventually he was blackballed from the club, a move supported by Savannah's parents. To retaliate, Oscar had accused the Drake family of "hanging papers," a term neither Josiah nor Cole had heard before.

"Suppose Cliffy sired a litter of puppies," Savannah explained. "But for whatever reason, either because he isn't a champion or he's not a great specimen of the breed, or perhaps because he has a genetic issue, I put another dog's name on the registration papers. Buyers would believe they were getting a puppy sired by that 'more valuable' dog." She made air quotes, then hugged Cliffy again as if to apologize for using him in her example.

"That's fraud," Cole put in.

"Yes, and it's a horrible practice that happens more often than anyone wants to admit," Savannah continued. "It's also a terrible accusation to make against a breeder like my dad, who would have closed his kennel before doing something so reprehensible. We were all shocked when Ogden made the accusation. Dad filed a lawsuit against him for slander. But my brother died shortly after that, and they lost interest in pursuing the suit." Her voice trailed away as she seemed momentarily lost in the past. "After that, my parents raised a couple more litters to accommodate their waiting list, then retired. It took me several years to step back into that world."

Josiah reached over Cliffy and placed his arm around her shoulder. As they gazed into each other's eyes, Cole once again took Ashley's hand, and she didn't let go.

"What do you remember about that time?" Josiah asked quietly.

"When word got around that Cliffy was missing, Ogden showed up," Savannah said. "He apologized to my parents, to all of us, for everything that had happened and said he wanted to help. He organized the search and passed out flyers. He did as much if not more than anyone else. And yet all that time, he must have had Cliffy."

"How terrible," Cole said.

Savannah frowned. "Now that I think of it, he also offered to contact the microchip company. Instead of reporting him missing, he must have taken the opportunity to change Cliffy's owner information." She scoffed. "Who does something like that?"

"Someone without a heart," Ashley blurted. Her blood had begun to boil as soon as Savannah had told them about the hanging papers accusation, and she was steaming mad.

During her last year in veterinary school, a classmate's family had been on the other side of a hanging-papers controversy, when DNA tests proved that a puppy they'd purchased was sired by a different dog than the one listed on the pedigree. The breeder had closed her kennel, but the ramifications had been ongoing and heartbreaking. Each of the puppies suffered from a genetic disease passed along by the true sire. Families had fallen in love with puppies they believed to be free of the disease.

Ashley had been appalled as her classmate shared the details with their study group. Now she was freshly appalled to hear about the lost reputation of a caring breeder because of a false accusation.

"You're right, Ashley. He had no heart." Savannah sighed heavily. "I'm sorry he's dead—I wouldn't have wished that on him—but I'm glad to be taking Cliffy away from him."

"It is a kind of poetic justice," Josiah said.

"I suppose." Savannah placed her napkin beside her plate. "If you'll excuse me, I'd like to call my parents."

"Of course," Ashley said. "Take all the time you need."

"I'm going to text my buddy." Josiah tapped his phone's screen. "Tell him Oscar's real name. Maybe he falsely accused someone who wasn't as forgiving as the Drakes." He tapped at his phone, then set it back down. "Though there's another angle to all of this. When I went through Rylee's laptop, I found something that might explain what she was up to."

"What's that?" Ashley asked, intrigued.

Josiah shifted in his seat. "I was going to wait to say anything until I'd connected a couple more dots, but since Savannah knew Moore, I'll tell you what I found when she comes back."

"Will this new angle prove Rylee's innocence?" Ashley asked, hoping against hope that Josiah would say yes.

He took a deep breath before replying. "We know she stole the dogs. And we know she was at Moore's place on Tuesday morning. I think I found their connection." He shook his head and his voice cracked. "Maybe she did kill him." He dropped his head into his hands. "I don't know what to think anymore."

Huge raindrops plopped on the picnic table as Ashley shook crumbs from the tablecloth. Fortunately, they'd cleared the table as soon as the wind kicked up. While Cole scraped the grill, Josiah and Savannah busied themselves in the kitchen, loading the dishwasher and putting condiments away.

"Do you have any idea what Josiah found on Rylee's computer?" Ashley asked Cole as she hurriedly folded the cloth and took shelter under the back porch roof.

"Not a clue." He closed the lid on the grill and draped the scarlet-and-gray cover over it. He'd given her the grill cover, which was imprinted with the Ohio State University insignia, to commemorate her alma mater shortly after she'd bought the grill. "Whatever Josiah found seems to have shaken him up, though, so it must not be anything good."

"Wendy asked me about Rylee's phone call to Josiah. She wanted to be sure that Rylee hadn't lied about being run off the road by a motorcyclist."

"She didn't." The two words thudded in the space between them with the weight of a bowling ball. Cole obviously had no doubts at all that the call was genuine.

"Her scream. Those gunshots." Ashley shivered. "I've had nightmares about the whole thing."

Cole immediately stopped fiddling with the cover and drew Ashley into an embrace. She snuggled close, grateful for the moment. He'd made a quick stop at his condo to shower and change clothes before arriving for the cookout. She breathed deeply, inhaling the woodsy fragrance of his soap mingled with the tantalizing notes of his aftershave. His Holy Cross Ranger T-shirt, one of his favorites, fitted nicely on his muscular build. Multiple washings had softened the fabric, which felt smooth against her cheek.

"We haven't had enough alone time lately," he murmured. "Maybe we can plan something special to do this weekend."

"I'd like that," she agreed, though she wasn't sure how that would be possible when Rob had blocks of time carved out for Talons Grip to practice. For now, though, she put aside all the distractions and contented herself with resting in his arms and watching the storm. The rain, coming down harder now, beat a rhythm on the porch roof and chattered among the trees. Its music reminded Ashley that despite the disturbing mystery that clung to them and their friends, she and Cole were blessed to have found one another. In her heart, Ashley said a silent prayer of thanks.

Lightning flashed, arcing toward the earth, its brilliancy followed by the low rumble of thunder. Max, standing inside the patio door, let out two sharp barks. Ashley laughed. "Our cue to go inside."

"Crazy weather," Cole grumbled good-naturedly as he escorted Ashley into the dining room.

Josiah and Savannah stood on the other side of the kitchen counter with amused smiles.

"Would you like the two of us to leave the two of you alone?" Josiah teased.

"I'd like you to stop looking at us like that," Cole retorted.

"How can we help it? You two make the cutest couple," Savannah gushed. "I know this will sound totally bizarre, but—no, I shouldn't say it."

"You can't stop now." Josiah closed the dishwasher door and wiped his hands on a nearby towel. "Tell us."

Savannah's cheeks became pink. "I'm very sorry that your cousin was in that accident. I would never want her to be hurt or anything. But in a way, I'm glad she stole the dogs. Otherwise, I'd never have found Cliffy. I'd never have met any of you." She closed her eyes and released a slow sigh. "That makes me an awful person. I know it does."

"Romans 8:28. 'All things work together for good.'" Josiah placed his hand on Savannah's shoulder. "I'm glad we met too. Though I wouldn't have minded if the circumstances were different."

Savannah smiled at him. "Me neither."

"Would you like the two of us to leave the two of *you* alone?" Cole parroted, a smug expression on his face.

"Maybe." Josiah winked at Savannah, but then his smile faded. "Unfortunately, I should get back to the hospital. I've already been gone too long."

"You said you found a connection," Ashley reminded him, though she doubted he needed any reminders. "Can you stay long enough to tell us what you found on her laptop?"

Once again, Josiah's shoulders slumped as if he carried the weight of the world. In a way, he did—at least the weight of his and Rylee's world. "I checked her Internet history and found she spent a lot of time on a specific message board." Josiah glanced at Savannah. "All about the evils of breeding and showing pedigreed dogs."

"Are you kidding me?" Savannah blurted out.

"I'm afraid not." Josiah leaned against the sink and folded his arms. "Apparently Rylee got connected with some animal rights group. I can't find much information about it, but the message board has only been active for about three months. The moderator pulled Rylee into a separate chat and managed to push all the right buttons. Rylee embraced the propaganda and agreed that show dogs were exploited by their owners."

"Do you think Oscar was the moderator?" Cole asked.

"There's no way to know without accessing his computer," Josiah said. "The people who use these kinds of boards hide behind fake personas. I can identify Rylee's messages because I was on her laptop. In one of the last messages, the moderator asked Rylee if she had the courage to take action. To be part of the 'Puppy Liberation Plan.'" Josiah made air quotes. "Not surprisingly, she jumped at the chance."

"That's what they called it?" Savannah appeared as though she was about to be sick. "We don't exploit our dogs. They're our pets. Our babies." She pressed her fingers against her forehead, then folded her arms across her chest. "At least for most of us. It's breeders like Ogden Sadler who create the problems. They give all of us a bad name."

"And then a—" Josiah pressed his lips together as if to stop himself from saying something he shouldn't.

Savannah put her hand on his arm. "Then a tenderhearted young woman—"

"With no common sense," Josiah interjected.

"—gets in over her head," Savannah finished.

"And may spend the rest of her life in prison." Josiah's eyes reddened and he ducked his head.

"We'll pray that doesn't happen." Savannah snaked her arm around Josiah's.

Cliffy, who'd been stretched out on Max's dog bed, padded into the kitchen and pressed his muzzle against Josiah's leg. Josiah smiled weakly and stroked the boxer's ears.

Cole leaned against the counter. "Back to this Puppy Liberation Plan. You have the evidence that the moderator persuaded Rylee to steal the dogs. Where was she taking them?"

"None of the details of the plan were on the message board," Josiah said. "The moderator asked Rylee for her phone number and told her to expect a call. Rylee being Rylee, she posted it. Right there on the message board."

Ashley wished she knew what to do or say that would ease Josiah's burden. He had every right to be upset with his cousin. Rylee had been foolish to post her phone number, even if it was in a private chat.

"Don't you have her phone?" Cole asked. "Did you check the call history?"

"The first day I had it, I called the people she'd been in contact with the most. A couple of them said she had this big secret, but they had no idea what she was up to. After I found the message board, I checked the call history again."

"For numbers you thought were spam the first time," Cole said. "The ones without any contact info."

Josiah confirmed that with a nod. "I found two she'd been in contact with several times. One of those has been disconnected. The other one rings but is never answered."

Ashley gasped. "That means two other people are involved. But why wasn't that third person in the private chat?"

"I don't have an answer to that question," Josiah replied.

"I think it's a fairly good bet that Oscar was either the moderator or the mystery third person," Cole said. "Maybe when Rylee got to Oscar's house, they argued and somehow she ended up—" He clamped his mouth shut instead of finishing the sentence. Not that he needed to. Ashley was certain they could all finish his thought—*she ended up killing Oscar Moore.*

"Until there's solid proof of that, I'm going to believe that Moore was already dead. She couldn't leave Cliffy with a dead body, so she put him in the van. When she got back on the road, she called me." Josiah paused to take a breath. "We all know what happened next."

Ashley glanced at a clearly miserable Savannah. Even though she hadn't overheard Josiah's terrifying phone call from Rylee, she and Ashley had talked about it the previous night.

"That's who it had to be," Savannah said. "Whoever was on the motorcycle. He killed Ogden-slash-Oscar, hid somewhere in the house when Rylee showed up, then after she left, he—I don't know. Maybe he was afraid she'd figure it out or had seen something that would give him away, so he went after her." She looked hopefully at Josiah. "It could have happened like that, couldn't it?"

"It's possible." Josiah's phone buzzed, and he dug it from his pocket. "It's Dr. Quinn. Excuse me." He stepped away from the group to take the call.

Ashley prayed that the medical director was calling with positive news. Rylee's brief bouts of consciousness had been encouraging, but she hadn't been alert enough to answer questions about the accident or about Oscar Moore. From what Josiah had said, she didn't seem to remember much of what had happened to her.

As Josiah listened to Dr. Quinn's news, his shoulders relaxed. A small smile tugged at his lips then spread into a full-fledged grin. "That's great news. I'll be right over. Thanks for calling."

Josiah's side of the conversation electrified the room. Cole pulled Ashley into a warm side hug and Savannah's eyes sparkled with happiness. Josiah ended the call and took a deep, cleansing breath as he gazed at them.

"Rylee is awake. Completely, fully awake." He started to pocket his phone, but it almost slid down the side of his shorts instead. He caught it, tried again, patted his pocket to ensure it was safe, then ran both hands through his short crop of hair as if he didn't know what else to do with them. "My prayers are answered. All our prayers."

He let out a whoop, then spontaneously grabbed Savannah and twirled her around the small kitchen space. Her excited giggle sparked laughter from Ashley and Cole. When Josiah placed Savannah back on her feet, their hands touched and remained clasped.

"I need to get over there." Josiah's words rushed over one another. "Before Chief Maloney questions her. I respect the chief, but I don't want her talking to him without an attorney."

Ashley started to tell Josiah that he needed to tell the police about the connection he'd found, because it could help them solve Oscar's murder.

But Cole interrupted her with the name of someone who would most certainly not condone sharing evidence with the police that could jeopardize his client's case. "I'll call Hector Slade on the way."

"You're coming with me?" Josiah asked.

"You bet we are," Cole replied. "We're standing with you on this, buddy. That's what friends do."

Minutes later, they were on their way to the medical center. Ashley went with Cole while Savannah rode with Josiah. Cole's call to Hector Slade, the defense attorney whose offices were on the second floor of the renovated fire station, went to voice mail.

"Hi, Hector," he said. "This is Cole Hawke. A friend of mine needs your help. Her name is Rylee Goodwin, and she just regained consciousness after being injured in an accident. Please call me as soon as you can. Thanks."

While Cole drove, Ashley stared through the windshield at Josiah's taillights, blurred by the falling rain. They were one step closer to puzzling out Rylee's role in the dog theft and her relationship with Oscar Moore.

Ashley prayed Savannah's scenario was right, and that Josiah's discovery didn't spell even more trouble for his cousin.

17

Dr. Dennis Quinn met the group in the lobby. "Rylee is asking for you," he told Josiah in his trademark deep, calming voice. "I promised her I'd take you to her as soon as you arrived."

"I'm sorry I wasn't here when she woke up," Josiah responded. "I should have been."

"Pardon my frankness, but I'm glad you weren't." The doctor offered a kind smile. "We were able to take care of Rylee's personal needs and evaluate her physical capabilities. Tolerance for food and things like that."

"She's eaten?" Josiah asked.

"A bit of broth and some orange sherbet."

"Her favorite, if I remember right." Josiah's smile grew even wider.

"She said the same." Dr. Quinn swept his gaze around the group. "I'm sorry, but I can only allow two of you to see her at a time."

They each murmured their understanding of the visitation policy while Josiah appeared deep in thought. "Ashley," he finally said. "Will you go with me?"

Surprised by the invitation, Ashley stammered her reply. "I'm happy to. But why me?"

"Because Cole has told me about the mysteries you've solved since moving to Aspen Falls. And because I know Chief Maloney trusts you." Josiah gave a sheepish grin. "Rylee is family. I'm not sure I can be entirely objective in this case. At least not yet. But you can be."

"I'm glad to go with you," Ashley said. "As long as you don't think Rylee will mind."

"She won't," Josiah reassured her. "I've talked so much about you and Cole. She already considers you a friend."

"That's settled then." Dr. Quinn gestured toward the interior double doors. "If you'll come with me."

When they reached the room, Dr. Quinn left them. Ashley lingered near the door while Josiah hurried to his cousin's side.

Rylee's short hair, unnaturally black with pink streaks, framed a pale, elfish face. She sat partially upright in the bed and tears flowed down her cheeks as Josiah gave her an awkward, gentle embrace.

"Look at you." He grabbed a tissue and handed it to her. "Everything is going to be okay. I promise."

"You don't know what I've done," Rylee said, her voice forlorn and sorrowful.

"That can wait. First I want you to meet someone." Josiah gestured toward the door. "This is Ashley Hart, my veterinarian friend. She's been praying for your recovery as much as I have."

Ashley stepped closer and smiled. "It's good to finally meet you."

"Is it?" Rylee bowed her head. "I thought I was doing the right thing. But when I saw C.G. and all that blood, I panicked. He was supposed to take the dogs. To find new homes for them where they could be pets instead of beauty pageant contestants. But I couldn't leave them there. Not when he was . . ." She rolled onto her side, tucking in her knees and drawing the blanket up to her face. "I wish I was still asleep. That I could sleep forever."

Josiah rubbed her shoulder. "We can talk about the dogs later."

"Are they okay?" Rylee asked, her voice muffled by the blanket. "Please tell me they're okay."

"Don't sugarcoat it," Josiah told Ashley quietly.

Ashley nodded. With Rylee fully aware of her surroundings, Josiah wanted her to understand the enormity of her actions—and their consequences. Ashley also wanted to talk to the young woman about the "beauty pageant" comment, but that conversation could wait.

"They were all frightened." In a soft but firm tone, Ashley told Rylee the details of how they'd found each of the dogs.

"Thankfully there's not much traffic on that road and none of them were hit," Josiah added. Apparently he had a tough love agenda. Though it could be what Rylee needed, Ashley preferred a gentler approach.

And yet, it wasn't the first time Rylee had engaged in reckless behavior. Her previous punishments—small fines and community service hours—had done nothing to keep her from once again involving herself in a questionable cause with little merit. She faced criminal charges for her role in the dog thefts, and she might face civil lawsuits too. The consequences were much graver. Given all that, Ashley could understand why Josiah needed his cousin to accept responsibility and grow up.

"Rugby, the papillon, injured his back," Ashley said. "And Ashes is still in my clinic because of injuries to his leg."

Quiet sobs shook Rylee's body. The sight of her, small and helpless under the stiff blanket, touched Ashley's heart. "I wanted to save them, not hurt them."

"Maybe this isn't the time," Ashley whispered to Josiah.

"It may be all the time we have," he responded.

Rylee shifted and pulled the blanket from her face, using it to wipe her cheeks at the same time. Her large hazel eyes were fixed on Josiah. "What do you mean by that? Are you leaving me?"

"Never," he said. "I know you're upset and you need to rest. To heal. But when the chief of police finds out you're awake, he's going to want to see you. He may already be on his way."

"I understand." Rylee's voice wavered. "I'll tell him everything I know. Except I don't know who shot at me or why he killed C.G."

Josiah's eyes narrowed. "The motorcyclist killed C.G.?"

"Didn't he?" Rylee asked.

"We don't know. Do you?" Josiah leaned closer to her. "Did you see him do it?"

Rylee recoiled and again drew the blanket to her chin as if to shield herself from Josiah's question. "C.G. was dead when I got there. I didn't see anybody."

Josiah examined her face, then released a long breath. "Rylee, I need to ask you something. It's very important you tell me the truth, no matter how bad it is. No matter how much you don't want to."

"Okay." Her eyes rounded, and the hazel irises darkened to a muddy brown.

"That man you call C.G.? His name was Oscar Moore," Josiah explained. "That is, people around here knew him by that name. His real name was Ogden Sadler. I have to know the truth, Rylee. Did you kill him?"

Rylee's lower lip trembled. "Is that what people think? Is that what the police think?"

Instead of answering, Josiah folded her hands between his.

"No." The primal pain in Rylee's voice was heart-wrenching. "No."

"I believe you." Josiah drew Rylee into another embrace as more sobs wracked her frail body. "Everything is going to be okay. I promise."

Ashley slipped from the room and leaned against the corridor wall. Rylee had done something foolish and immature. Even stupid. And she was in a world of trouble because of it. But she hadn't murdered Oscar Moore. Ashley was certain of that.

Hopefully Chief Maloney would believe in her innocence too.

Chief Dan Maloney and Deputy Chief Jana Lewis arrived at the hospital shortly after Rylee had stopped crying and was savoring another cup of orange sherbet.

Josiah made introductions, then asked the chief if Ashley could stay. When Ashley glanced at Rylee, the young woman's eyes filled with tears again.

"I'd like you to stay too," she said. "That is, if you don't hate me."

"Of course I don't hate you," Ashley reassured her. "Though I'm not very happy about what you did."

"I know." Rylee set the half-eaten sherbet cup on the bedside tray. "I'm not proud of what I did either. Not anymore."

Deputy Chief Lewis stepped forward and cleared her throat. She wore a light-gray cropped jacket and matching slacks instead of her usual uniform, and her voice was authoritative but kind. "What exactly did you do, Rylee?"

"Hold on a sec." Josiah held up a hand. "Cole left a message for Hector Slade. I'm not comfortable with Rylee answering any questions until he gets here."

Rylee reached for his hand. "I know I shouldn't have taken the dogs, Josey. But I didn't kill C.G. Until they find who did, I'll always be a suspect. I want to help."

Josiah took a deep breath and shifted his gaze to Ashley as if seeking her advice.

"I can't tell you what to do," she said. "But I do know that Chief Maloney and Deputy Chief Lewis want justice, not a scapegoat. Whoever killed Oscar—or Ogden, or whatever his name was—needs to be put in prison."

Josiah studied the two chiefs as if assessing them in light of

Ashley's answer, then he turned to Dr. Quinn, who'd escorted them into the room. "What do you think, doctor?"

Dr. Quinn studied the monitor, then placed his fingers on Rylee's wrist. Since her pulse reading was on the monitor, Ashley guessed he was buying time to consider his answer.

"Please, doctor?" Rylee pleaded. "I'm fine. I promise."

"Okay," Dr. Quinn reluctantly agreed and pointed to the monitor. "But if any of those numbers go wacky, I reserve the right to stop the interview."

Rylee smiled and her hazel eyes brightened with amusement. "Is 'wacky' a medical term?"

"Indeed it is," Dr. Quinn replied. "Ask your questions, officers. I'll monitor Ms. Goodwin's heart rate from the nurses station."

After the doctor left, Lewis eyed Josiah, who nodded his go-ahead. The deputy chief stepped closer to the bed. "Tell me about the dogs," she said in a warm, conversational tone.

Chief Maloney, his authoritative demeanor made more intimidating by his large size, stayed near the door. They had probably discussed a plan of action before arriving, and the approachable yet whip-smart Lewis had been tasked with conducting the interview.

Rylee began her story by talking about the message board she'd found for a new animal rights group. Their approach wasn't to draw attention to themselves with large and noisy protests against, in the organizer's words, "poor breeding practices and senseless beauty pageants." Instead, anonymous strike teams of two or three members were tasked to disrupt the lives of specially selected show dog owners. The objective of the Puppy Liberation Plan was to steal certain dogs who'd competed at a dog show in Colorado Springs.

"Who were the members of your team?" Lewis asked.

"We used code names," Rylee replied. "I didn't know C.G.'s real name until Josiah told me. They called me Flush. That was the name of Elizabeth Barrett Browning's dog. He was dognapped at least three times."

"Elizabeth Barrett Browning the poet?" Josiah asked.

"Yup." Rylee leaned back against the pillow.

"I've read about this," Ashley said. "Elizabeth paid a ransom each time to the same man, a guy called Taylor. He pretended to negotiate between the dognappers and their victims. But Taylor was probably involved in the thefts."

"In a fictionalized version of London's dognapping ring, Taylor was called Ginger," Rylee explained. "So Ginger was the code name for the other person in our group."

Josiah shook his head. "Seems a strange source for code names. Why would anyone want to be associated with those kinds of thieves?"

"Why C.G.?" Ashley asked.

"C.G. stands for Chelsea George. He was a professional dognapper at the same time as Taylor."

"Tell me more about Ginger," Deputy Chief Lewis said, steering the interview back to the important facts.

"She stole the dogs from the show," Rylee explained. "We met at a rest area and traded vehicles. My job was to take the dogs to C.G."

"And you don't know her name?" Lewis asked.

Rylee shook her head. "I only knew her as Ginger."

"The van you were driving is registered to Valerie Nelson," the deputy chief continued. "Is that name familiar to you?"

Rylee shook her head. "No."

"She says you stole the van from her," Lewis said.

Rylee's cheeks flushed. "I didn't *steal* it," she protested. "I mean, technically I did, but that was all part of the plan. Ginger stole it first so she'd have a vehicle roomy enough for all the dogs."

Chief Maloney stepped forward. "Ms. Nelson had a contract with the owners to transport the dogs back to Amarillo. In her statement to the Colorado State Police, she said she stopped at the rest area for a break. She left the van running while she went inside, and when she came back to the parking area, her van was gone."

"I don't understand." Rylee's confused expression made her look even more vulnerable.

"I think I do." Josiah shifted his gaze from his cousin to Lewis. "Do you have a photo of Valerie Nelson?"

Jana opened her electronic tablet, tapped the screen, and showed the image to Rylee.

"That's Ginger," Rylee said. "I watched her get out of the van."

"This is Ms. Nelson's driver's license photo," the deputy chief said. "She lives in Texas."

Ashley, who stood on the opposite side of Rylee's bed, stared at the photo as indignation coursed through her. "That means she was in on it. She even had the nerve to come to the clinic and demand I give her the dogs." Not to mention the confrontation with Savannah in the coffee shop during which Valerie pretended to be a victim too.

The blood seemed to leave Rylee's face, and tears welled in her eyes.

Josiah squeezed her hand. "They should have code-named you Patsy," he said with a gentle smile. "It sounds to me like you were set up to be the fall guy—or in this case, the fall girl—if things went sideways."

"Which they did," Chief Maloney said, stepping forward. "Now let's talk about C.G."

The door suddenly flung open and Hector Slade burst into the room, followed closely by Dr. Quinn.

"Don't say a word, young lady," Hector warned. "Not another word until you and I have had a chance to talk."

"Ms. Goodwin has had quite enough excitement for now," Dr. Quinn added. "She needs her rest."

Ashley said a quick goodbye, then accompanied Chief Maloney and Deputy Chief Lewis to the waiting room while Josiah stayed with Rylee and Hector. The receptionist directed them to the cafeteria, where they found Cole and Savannah, both eager to hear what had happened.

"First things first," Chief Maloney said. "We need to get a BOLO out on this Valerie Nelson."

"I'll take care of that," Lewis said, stepping away from the table to call Angie Sherman, the receptionist at the police department. The "be on the lookout" request would soon be forwarded to other law enforcement agencies around the state and in Texas.

When Lewis returned to the group, Ashley and Savannah recounted their conversations with Valerie.

Chief Maloney listened carefully and asked a few clarifying questions. When they'd finished, he leaned back in his chair. "Assuming Rylee is telling the truth, I think Josiah was right," he said. "Ms. Nelson set Rylee up to take the fall if anything went wrong with the Puppy Liberation Plan. It's one person's word against the other's, and we know Rylee isn't innocent."

"We need evidence tying Ms. Nelson to the dognapping," Jana said. "Otherwise, she might not be held accountable."

"I, for one, don't believe Valerie is a victim." Savannah crossed her arms. "Maybe she's the one who killed Ogden. Oscar. Whatever you want to call him."

"Rylee calls him C.G.," Ashley said.

Cole humphed. "The man of many names. Ogden Sadler. Oscar Moore. Ansel Dodger." He grinned. "That one is my favorite because that's exactly who he was. He dodged his fans. In a way, he dodged nearly everyone in Aspen Falls. Not to mention how he managed to dodge responsibility for what he did to Savannah and her family."

"Say those names again," Ashley said as she retrieved a small notepad and pen from her bag.

Cole gave her a quizzical look but complied.

Ashley scribbled the name *Ogden Sadler* on a clean sheet of paper. "Now watch this."

Everyone leaned in closer as she wrote out the letters for *Ansel Dodger* one at a time. As she wrote the *A* for Ansel, she crossed out the *a* in Sadler. She did the same with the other letters.

"See?" She triumphantly held up the paper. "His pseudonym is an anagram."

"He always was a pompous narcissist," Savannah proclaimed. "I just wish I'd figured that out when I first saw one of his books. We'd have had Cliffy home again a long time ago, and Ogden would have paid a heavy price for what he did to my family."

Ashley didn't know if Savannah was right about that. After all, the reclusive author had spent years safeguarding his privacy. The few people he let in on the secret, such as Katee Havenstar, knew him as Oscar Moore instead of his given name.

Suddenly, something that Rylee had said popped into Ashley's mind.

We were to disrupt the lives of specially selected show dog owners.

Specially selected, such as Savannah Drake? Did Oscar Moore still hold a grudge against the Drake family—one that festered despite his theft of Cliffy? Perhaps the entire animal rights organization was a sham made up by Oscar to cause Savannah more grief.

Such a plot seemed too crazy. Too implausible. Yet Ashley had been involved in quite a few crazy, implausible mysteries since moving to Aspen Falls.

Her imagination shifted into overdrive. What if Savannah *had* figured out the secret of the anagram?

Ogden would have paid a heavy price for what he did to my family.

What if, somehow, Savannah was the murderer?

There I go again, letting my imagination go crazy.

Ashley's ridiculous notion of her new friend as a murderer melted away in less time than a snowflake on a hot stove. No one as gracious and compassionate as Savannah could possibly take the life of another human being. But that left one question.

Who had?

18

The rain continued throughout the night, at times loud and thunderous, and other times soft and soothing. The temperamental weather echoed the events of the past week, Ashley mused Saturday morning as she grated cheese to top the egg casserole she was making.

Sometimes frightening, such as Josiah's phone call from Rylee and the discovery of Oscar Moore's dead body.

Sometimes gentle, like the private looks exchanged between Savannah and Josiah, between Ashley and Cole, and even between long-and-happily-married Lorie and Rob Tavish.

Sometimes comforting, such as the affection shown to stranded dogs by their foster families and the affection Cliffy had for Josiah, which made the handsome bachelor even more appealing to Savannah.

"You can trust the man your dog trusts," Savannah had said during one of their late-night conversations. Ashley agreed with her. Max had loved Cole since the first day they met. And Ashley had noticed.

Shortly after she put the egg casserole in the oven, the man who had won both her and Max's hearts arrived with an assortment of pastries from Three Peaks Bakery. He greeted Ashley with a kiss, then glanced around the kitchen. "Where's Max?"

"Josiah and Savannah took Max and Cliffy on a mountain drive." Savannah planned to drive to Vail with the show dogs in a few hours to meet her pilot friend, so Ashley had encouraged her and Josiah to spend some time together alone before Savannah left town.

Ashley retrieved a decorative serving tray from a lower cabinet and transferred the pastries from the bakery box.

"That was thoughtful of them to take both those big boys." Cole popped a grape from the fruit bowl into his mouth. "I don't think I've ever been here without Max. It doesn't feel right."

"I feel the same way. But Cliffy is happiest when he's with one of them, and since he was going, Max thought he should go too. Besides, getting those two out of the house while I prep for brunch was the best way for Savannah to help. I didn't have much planned, so cooking is a one-person job this morning."

"Make that one and a half. I'll supervise." Cole winked at Ashley and took a few more grapes. "Who all is coming to this brunch?"

"The foster families, Holly and Ryan, and Lorie and Rob. Jen is stopping by to drop off Ashes, but Ellen and Ben both had other plans so they can't make it. There may be others I don't even know about."

"Sounds like half the town is going to be here."

"I think Savannah would have invited the entire town if I'd had a bigger house." Ashley handed him the completed tray to place on the buffet table in the dining area. "This brunch is her way of thanking the families and the new friends she made here."

"I know one new friend who's especially unhappy to see her go. Josiah W Hunter."

"What does the W stand for?"

"Nothing." Cole grinned. "That W doesn't even get a period."

Ashley narrowed her eyes in skepticism. "You're teasing me."

Cole chuckled. "I'm not. He's like Harry Truman, whose parents gave him the middle name S to honor his grandfathers. It wasn't an initial, just part of his name."

"Actually, I think I knew that."

The front door opened. "We're coming in," Holly sang out from the entry.

"Please do." Ashley entered the great room to greet her best friend with a warm hug. "I feel like I haven't seen you in days."

"You've been busy with another mystery." Holly handed Cole a long wicker basket holding a hot casserole dish as he and Ryan greeted each other. "That's my world-famous Italian sausage casserole. It needs to bake for about ten more minutes."

Ashley glanced at her watch. "Will you set it on the stove for now?" she asked Cole. "I'll stick it in the oven in about five minutes so the casseroles finish at the same time."

"Where's the guest of honor?" Holly asked. "She stopped by 3 Alarm Fur with Ashes yesterday. What a sweetheart that little guy is. And so is she. Maybe she'll find a reason to visit us again."

Ashley chuckled at Holly's exuberance. "She may have. Josiah took her for a drive so they could spend some time together before she leaves."

Holly's eyes gleamed with speculation. "If she had let me do the matchmaking, he's exactly who I would have chosen for her."

Ashley chuckled again, then greeted Gwen and Pastor Adam Vance, who arrived with Rugby and another dish to add to the buffet. Josiah and Savannah returned next, followed by the Heaths and Bridey. More guests, along with the other dogs, weren't far behind.

When the impressive spread was ready, the guests stood around the table before serving themselves. Savannah expressed her thanks to those who opened their homes to Bridey and the other dogs, and all those who had made her feel so welcome. Cole held Ashley's hand while Pastor Vance gave a blessing. When he prayed for Rylee's healing, Ashley couldn't resist sneaking a peek at Josiah—in time to see Savannah, with her head bent and her eyes closed, take his hand.

No doubt about it. Savannah would definitely be coming back to Aspen Falls.

The minutes passed quickly as everyone enjoyed the delicious food and wonderful company. As the morning slipped past noon, the sun emerged and chased the rain clouds away. The guests said their farewells and wished Savannah well on her trip home. The foster families were used to having a dog or cat with them for just a short time, but they still lingered over their goodbyes to their four-legged guests.

Except for the Heaths. They were first-time fosters, and Andie was having an especially hard time saying goodbye to Bridey. The teenager and Savannah sat together on the couch in deep conversation, the Cavalier spaniel tucked between them, while Wendy and Holly helped Ashley clean the kitchen. Rich, Ryan, Cole, and Josiah were outside situating crates and portable carriers in Savannah's rental vehicle.

"What's going to happen to Cliffy?" As a police officer, Wendy knew all about Oscar Moore's prior connection to the Drake family. Ashley had also told Holly that the boxer belonged to Savannah.

"I'm still waiting on the results of the DNA test," Ashley said. "When they arrive, we'll compare them to the info I received from the Drakes."

"Do you have any doubts he's Savannah's dog?" Wendy asked as she scraped the bottom of one of the casserole dishes.

"None whatsoever," Ashley said confidently. "But Savannah's attorney strongly advised her not to take any legal action until we have evidence. Even then, he suggests she discuss the ownership issue with the executor of Oscar's estate before trying to claim him."

Holly frowned thoughtfully. "Who is the executor, by the way?"

"That's another mystery." Ashley closed the lid on a shallow bowl of leftovers from a charcuterie board that Savannah had ordered from Holliday's Mountain Market. "Savannah asked Hector Slade about it before he left the hospital last night. Since Oscar seemed to do most of his shopping in Beaver Creek, Hector said he'd talk to an attorney there."

"What if Oscar doesn't have a will?" Holly asked.

"In that case, Max will have a roommate until we can figure something out." Ashley didn't tell the other ladies about the confidential news Savannah had passed along to her earlier. The morning drive into the mountains had included a visit to a rental property that Josiah had his eyes on—ten wooded acres nestled in a narrow valley. The owner was open to selling, and Josiah planned to make an offer. Once he moved from his pet-unfriendly room at The Hitching Post, he could take Cliffy. As much as Savannah loved the boxer, she knew he'd be happier in the country than in her tiny condominium.

The men entered the house, and Rich crouched beside Andie. "It's time for us to go, sweetheart. Savannah needs to be on her way."

Andie nodded, her face set in stone as she struggled to hold in her emotions.

Savannah put her arm around the teen. "You can lead Bridey to the car if you want."

"I'd like that," Andie said.

The other dogs had already been loaded up, leaving only Bridey and Savannah's rolling suitcase, which Josiah took charge of, to take out to the waiting SUV. As soon as Bridey was in her carrier and Andie had given Savannah a hug, the Heaths said their goodbyes. They walked to their car with Andie between them.

"Andie doesn't know it yet," Savannah said, watching the family drive away, "but she is getting her own Cavalier King Charles spaniel after this murder mess is settled. Wendy is hesitant to take a gift from me until then because of, as she put it, 'my past relationship with the deceased.'"

Though excited for Andie, Ashley was taken aback at the implication. "Wendy can't think you had anything to do with Oscar's death. You weren't even in town." Though, remembering her own momentary suspicion, she realized that if the thought had occurred to her, no matter how briefly, it must have occurred to Wendy too.

"She doesn't," Savannah said in her usual confident tone. "But she's also concerned about any appearance of impropriety. I totally understand that." She faced Ashley and grabbed both of her hands. "Thank you so much for opening your home to me. For all you've done. I'll never be able to repay you."

"I loved having you," Ashley replied. "Come anytime."

Savannah laughed, and her gaze darted to Josiah. "I'm going to hold you to that invitation."

Ashley smiled. "I hope you do."

The two women hugged, then Savannah embraced Holly. Cole and Ryan also said their goodbyes, both of them accepting a mischievous peck on the cheek from the auburn-haired beauty before she joined Josiah at her vehicle. She turned to wave goodbye one last time, then Ashley, Cole, and the Kipps went inside the house where Max and Cliffy awaited them.

Josiah came in a few minutes later. From the buoyant spring in his step and the hint of lip color near his mouth, he'd received a farewell kiss he wouldn't soon forget.

With the dogs finally on their way home, Ashley felt a weight lifted from her shoulders. The mystery of the murder still remained, but Rylee's health was improving. She had legal challenges ahead of her, but she also had a competent defense attorney with a well-deserved reputation for working miracles.

If only they could find Valerie Nelson. She was obviously involved with the theft of the dogs. Had she also killed Oscar? Ashley wished she knew the answer to that impossible question.

19

After the Friday night drama at the hospital, a whirlwind day on Saturday, and church Sunday morning, Ashley looked forward to a long and lazy afternoon alone at home with Max and Cliffy for company.

Granted, she wouldn't have traded Saturday's fun and joy for more rest. She loved having a houseful of company, a buffet table overflowing with delicious foods, and laughter echoing from every corner. The eight dogs of varying sizes had added to the festive atmosphere. Josiah, still a relative newcomer, and Savannah had been treated like long-lost friends, just as Ashley herself had been not too long before.

Not that there wasn't sadness too. Even though Rylee was a stranger, everyone seemed genuinely concerned for her well-being. Then there was Andie, brokenhearted at saying goodbye to Bridey. Ashley hoped that Wendy would eventually allow Savannah to give the teen a puppy of her own.

Naturally, gossip abounded, especially concerning Oscar Moore. His identity as Ansel Dodger was no longer a secret, nor was the fact that he'd lived among them, a neighbor—albeit a reclusive one—as someone he wasn't. The prominent theory was that someone from his past life as Ogden Sadler had discovered his whereabouts and exacted vengeance for a long-ago grievance.

Ashley had to admit that such talk bothered her since Savannah was the one person in Aspen Falls who had known Oscar as Ogden, and she certainly had a grievance against him. But the idea of Savannah as a seeker of revenge was too preposterous to take seriously.

A few minutes after Savannah left, Josiah had gone to the hospital to be with Rylee during her meeting with Chief Maloney. Thankfully, Hector was there too.

Ashley and Cole had spent the rest of Saturday with the Kipps. Another downpour kept them inside, playing games and snacking most of the day. In the evening, they'd ordered pizza and watched a movie before calling it a night.

After changing from her church dress into yoga pants and an old veterinary conference T-shirt, Ashley curled up on the couch with a popular women's magazine. While a romantic comedy played on the television, her mind drifted from one thing to another and eventually landed on the realization that she'd forgotten something important. It was the same feeling she'd had earlier that week, on Thursday when she'd been on her farm rounds.

But whatever nibbled on the edges of her brain was too nebulous to grasp. Her mind drifted again until the magazine slipped from her fingers and her eyes refused to stay open another second.

Her long and lazy Sunday afternoon abruptly ended around four o'clock when the buzzing of her phone woke her from the much-needed nap. Deputy Chief Jana Lewis's name appeared on the phone's screen. Ashley brushed the sleep from her eyes and answered with a cheery hello. No need for the deputy chief to know she'd been napping.

"Sorry to bother you," Lewis said, her voice crisp and clear through the speaker. "Chief Maloney wants to know if you could come to the station. We got some interesting results back from the crime lab and want to go over all the evidence again, including your statement."

"My statement?" Ashley echoed. "I don't think there's anything else I can tell you that you don't already know."

"We need a signed statement about Valerie Nelson's visit to the clinic," the deputy chief explained. "It might not mean anything, but in cases like this, you never can say ahead of time what's important and what isn't."

"I totally understand." Ashley rose from the couch. "I'll be there in about fifteen to twenty minutes."

"Great. See you soon."

"You know what this means, don't you, Max?" Ashley asked the Dalmatian as he followed her to the bedroom. "The police are building a case against Valerie, which means that the crime unit must have found something important. And that means Rylee will no longer be a suspect in the murder."

Max warbled his unique vocalization, which Ashley interpreted as shared enthusiasm.

Truly, it would be a blessing for Rylee's name to be cleared. She'd likely still be charged with the dog thefts, and rightly so, but Ashley hoped that the sentencing wouldn't be too harsh. Though she hadn't seen Rylee since Friday night, Josiah had mentioned in church that morning that his young cousin was prepared to face the consequences of her actions and had vowed to never get involved in anything so foolish again.

He'd also confided that Savannah planned to smooth matters over with the other dog owners as much as possible. She hoped, with Hector's help, to negotiate a settlement that would avoid any civil suits. In her proposed plan, Rylee would be required to pay all vet bills and perhaps make a donation or commit volunteer hours to Fluffy Friends. The owners might add additional provisions to any agreement, but Savannah believed their anger would be focused on Valerie, the person who'd been entrusted with the safety of their dogs in the first place. Because of her betrayal, she'd no doubt take most of the blame.

When Ashley arrived at town hall, she parked beside Josiah's vehicle. The building housed police headquarters, plus the mayor's office, post office, and other government services, but those were all closed on Sundays. At least she was parked close enough to the entrance to make a run for it through the gentle rain.

Deputy Chief Lewis met Ashley in the lobby. They made small talk about the weather as Lewis led the way to a small conference room. Josiah and Chief Maloney rose from their seats as the women entered and greetings were exchanged.

When everyone was settled, Chief Maloney closed the door. "First of all, I want to thank you both for coming in on this rainy Sunday afternoon," he said. "It's been a long week for everybody, including those experts in the crime unit who worked overtime to give us some answers."

"I want to do whatever I can to prove Rylee's innocence in the murder," Josiah said. "But the crime lab now has her laptop and phone, plus all my notes. I'm not sure what else I can tell you." He had given the devices to Chief Maloney late Friday night after he and Rylee had talked to Hector. Since Rylee had already confessed to her role in the dog theft, the defense attorney thought it important that they cooperate with law enforcement in every way possible.

Ashley understood Josiah's confusion. Lewis's request for a review of Ashley's statement seemed more like an excuse to get her to come to the station instead of a genuine reason. So why was she here?

"We appreciate your cooperation," Chief Maloney said to Josiah. "Especially since handing in that evidence implicates your cousin. I'm surprised Hector Slade allowed it."

"You have Rylee's confession," Josiah said. "She has nothing to hide."

A cold chill raced up Ashley's spine as the chief and deputy chief exchanged glances. "You said the crime unit gave you answers," she said. "Are you able to tell us what they are?"

"Actually, that's why we wanted to see both of you," Lewis replied.

"This may be a little unorthodox, but we think your input can help us." She paused to take a deep breath. "After all, Josiah was a criminal investigator in the army, and though Ashley is an amateur sleuth, she's a smart and intuitive one."

"We want to tell you what we know," Chief Maloney put in. "Maybe by working together, we can figure out what happened to Oscar Moore. To be clear, though, anything said in this room stays in this room. I need that assurance from both of you."

Ashley and Josiah readily agreed.

Chief Maloney leaned forward. "Perhaps the most important news is that a sharp-eyed off-duty police officer spotted Valerie Nelson at a diner outside Denver yesterday afternoon. We have her in a holding cell in the basement."

Josiah appeared as shocked as Ashley felt. "What is she saying?" he asked.

"That she's innocent," the chief replied. "Rylee stole her van and the dogs. She doesn't know Oscar by that or any other name. And she's blaming you." He gestured toward Josiah.

"Me?" Taken aback by the accusation, Josiah's eyes darted from the chief to Ashley and back again. "She doesn't even know me."

Deputy Chief Lewis tapped her fingers on the closed folder in front of her. "She apparently learned a great deal of information during her brief sojourn in Aspen Falls. She's accusing you of protecting Rylee by shifting the blame to her. And she says that she's going to sue you, Savannah, Ashley, and the entire town." She humphed. "I'd like to see her try that nonsense."

"How can she sue me?" Ashley asked. "Or anyone?"

"She likes to hear herself talk," Lewis said. "You don't need to worry about her."

Easier said than done. Ashley was aware that anyone could sue anyone else for just about anything. But she knew she'd been right to keep the dogs' whereabouts a secret from Valerie.

Chief Maloney slid the folder from his deputy to Josiah. "The crime lab is still digging through the message board. It might take a few days to tie Valerie to any of the participants. But they did a rush job on a couple of tests. Take a peek."

Josiah opened the folder and scanned the first page. He shot a smile in Ashley's direction. "Valerie Nelson's fingerprints were found in Oscar's kitchen."

"So she was there." Ashley's brow furrowed. "But she said she didn't know him."

"She lied," Lewis said, her lips spreading into a self-satisfied smile. "The problem is that we don't know *when* she was there."

Josiah flipped to another page in the folder. "She had a gun?"

"In her handbag," Chief Maloney said.

"The same gun was used to fire the bullet found in the van's tire." Josiah raised his eyes from the report. "She was the motorcyclist?"

"Again, we don't know," Lewis said. "Could Rylee have killed Oscar?" When Josiah started to object, she raised her hand to stop him. "Please put on your investigator cap and hear me out on this. Could Rylee have killed Oscar? Maybe. She admits to being at the scene. Her fingerprints were found at the scene. Oscar's blood was on her shirt, in the van, and on the boxer's paws."

Ashley's eyes widened at that last bit of information. It was the first she'd heard of those results, though she supposed it was what she'd assumed all along.

"Could Valerie have killed Oscar?" the deputy chief continued. "Maybe. She denies even knowing the man, but her fingerprints are in his house. She has a gun in her possession that was used to fire a bullet into the tire of the van. But Oscar wasn't killed with a gun."

"And simply because she has the gun doesn't mean she pulled the trigger," Josiah said, sounding defeated. "All the evidence on both sides is circumstantial."

"Unfortunately, it weighs heavier against Rylee," Chief Maloney said.

Ashley had been sitting silently, processing the information. Now she spoke up. "Except that Valerie lied. Deputy Chief, you said so yourself. But Rylee hasn't. She's cooperating. Doesn't that count for anything?"

"It does," the chief said. "Right now, with their conflicting stories, I don't think the district attorney could charge either one of them for the murder. I don't think he'd even charge Valerie for purposely running Rylee off the road. We need something, anything—and I'm sorry to say this, but I have to deal with the facts—that convicts one of them and exonerates the other."

"You need the murder weapon." Josiah's statement fell between them, and Ashley's stomach lurched.

"That would be helpful," the chief agreed.

"What about the motorcycle?" Ashley asked.

"We're searching for it," Lewis said. "But even if we find it, we won't be able to prove Valerie was following Rylee."

"There must be something we can do," Ashley said.

"We can go back to the basics." Josiah closed the folder and let it drop to the table. "Means, motive, and opportunity. Much as I hate to say it, both Rylee and Valerie had the means and the opportunity. They were both in the kitchen and the knife—if it's the one missing from the set on the counter—was accessible. But what is the motive? Rylee doesn't have one."

"Josiah is right," Ashley said. "Rylee was following the plan she'd been given. She took the van from the rest area and drove to Oscar's house to give him the dogs. What possible reason could she have to kill him?"

Lewis raised her hand. "Devil's advocate. What is Valerie's motive?"

"We don't know," Ashley said. "But we do know she wasn't supposed to be there. If she wasn't part of the dog theft plan, how did she even know Oscar? And if she was part of the plan, her role supposedly ended once Rylee drove away from the rest area."

"You're on to something there," the chief said. "Rylee told me yesterday that the teams were small and anonymous on purpose. She knew where to take the dogs, but 'Ginger' didn't. Otherwise, Ginger would have taken them to Oscar's house herself."

"We also need to consider the time line." Lewis tilted her head in thought. "Both women were in the kitchen. But which one got there first? Or were they there at the same time?"

Ashley pressed her fingers against her temples as the horrific memory of Rylee's phone call with Josiah reverberated in her head. *This guy. On a motorcy— . . . He's trying to kill me.*

"Rylee thought a man was on the motorcycle." She grabbed Josiah's arm. "She didn't even suspect that it might be Ginger because she'd left her at the rest stop."

Josiah stared at Ashley. "Which means Rylee didn't see Ginger at Oscar's house."

"Ginger, aka Valerie, was chasing Rylee." Ashley paused, trying to think through the logical sequence of events. "Because Rylee was at the house first." Her grip tightened on Josiah's arm. "When Valerie arrived, Oscar was dead. She knew Rylee had been there—"

"And she believes Rylee killed Oscar." Josiah's eyes widened.

"So she tried to kill Rylee because . . ." The answer came to Ashley as if it were written on the wall in large red letters. "Because Valerie was in love with Oscar."

"Or, more likely, obsessed," Josiah said. "I doubt she'd ever met him in real life. They communicated solely on the message board and by phone."

"Which means she followed Rylee to find out where he lived because Oscar only told Rylee. Not Valerie."

"Wait a minute." Chief Maloney held up both hands. "That's a fascinating theory the two of you have going there, but I need the bottom line. Which one of them killed Oscar Moore?"

Without a glance at each other, Ashley and Josiah answered in unison. "Neither of them."

20

Tuesday morning, the sun shone bright, scaring away the last of the rain clouds in the skies above Aspen Falls. It was the kind of day Ashley loved. The atmosphere clung to a bit of the rain, so the sun's rays didn't feel as hot as on a typical summer day. But the weather was still warm and bright with a freshness to the breeze. The birds seemed to sing louder, greeting the day and each other, after hiding away in the trees during the on-again, off-again showers.

Plus, farm rounds were more easily accomplished during sunny days instead of rainy ones. The farm lots might still be muddy, but at least neither Ashley nor the animals were being pelted by rain. The other benefit was that Max could go with her, and she didn't have to worry about having a wet dog in the front seat. She could wipe any mud or debris off his paws before he jumped in the back. However, since Ashley believed the philosophy of "an ounce of prevention is worth a pound of cure," she'd also covered the back seat with a fleece blanket she kept on hand for the specific purpose of Max-proofing her car.

Currently, she and Max were on their way to visit an alpaca herd for a follow-up visit with its newest member. A couple of weeks ago, the owners had bought Merry, a scraggly-looking brown-and-white female who'd been kept with a few goats in less-than-ideal conditions. Since alpacas needed to be with their own kind to thrive, it had been an impulsive purchase of the heart and, monetarily speaking, not a well-thought-out decision.

The owners didn't care. Merry, despite her aggressive spitting and tendency to hold her head at an angle, belonged to their herd now. Ashley had visited Merry the day after her arrival to her new home and diagnosed her with a severe ear infection, giving her antibiotics and pain medicine to help her heal.

Ashley crested a hill and noticed a mail truck stopped at a roadside mailbox. She slowed to pass the vehicle and waved at Merle Brooks. He lifted a hand in response, then returned to his task. Ashley had driven a few more winding miles when her mind finally grabbed hold of the nebulous thought that had been bugging her for days.

She glanced at the dashboard clock to confirm her suspicion.

"It doesn't make any sense," she said to Max, who grumbled a reply. "Merle was close to where I saw him last week. So why would he have been near Oscar's place at this time on the day of the murder?"

She braked to stop at the next intersection and, since nobody was behind her, allowed the Subaru to idle. Her mind needed a moment to channel her intuitive thoughts into a logical conclusion.

"If he wasn't at Oscar's, then he couldn't have seen the van." She stared at Max in the rearview mirror. He cocked his head as if understanding every word she said. "But if he didn't see the van, why did he say he did?"

Ashley didn't want to face the possible answer to that question.

After the meeting with Chief Maloney and Deputy Chief Lewis on Sunday, Ashley was convinced that neither Rylee nor Valerie had killed Oscar.

But if Rylee and Valerie were innocent, then who was the murderer?

Savannah Drake? Not likely.

Katee Havenstar? Never.

Ashley stared in her rearview mirror, gazing beyond Max out her back window. If she stayed at the intersection, Merle would catch up to her. Surely there was an explanation for Merle's change of route that day. All Ashley had to do was ask.

The buzz of her phone startled her from her reverie. She took a moment to catch her breath, then checked the screen.

Savannah.

"Guess where I am," Savannah said when Ashley answered. "You never will, so I might as well tell you."

With that kind of prompting, the guess was too easy. "You're back already? I can't say I'm surprised."

Savannah laughed. "I'll be in Aspen Falls in about fifteen minutes or so. Are you at the clinic?"

"I'm on my way to see an alpaca."

Silence.

"Savannah? Are you there?"

"Did you say an alpaca?" Wonder filled Savannah's voice. "I've always wanted to see a real live alpaca."

Ashley chuckled. "There's a herd east of town. I'm sure the owners wouldn't mind if you stopped by sometime."

"How about now, while you're there? Do you think that would be okay?"

Ashley took a moment to process the surprise request, then grinned. "Sure, why not? Are you driving in from Vail? If so, it's not that much of a detour."

"Yep," Savannah chirped. "My pilot friend needed to go back to Denver. So here I am. Can you text me the address?"

"Give me a sec." Ashley sent her the farm's address. "On its way."

"Got it," Savannah said a moment later. "This will be so much fun."

"Be warned. The alpaca I'm treating today is a notorious spitter." Ashley glanced in her rearview mirror as Merle's mail truck rounded a curve.

"I've never been spit on by an alpaca before." Savannah laughed. "Something to check off my bucket list."

"I've already checked it off mine." Ashley stared in the mirror as Merle stopped at the only house on this section of the road. "I need to go. Merle Brooks is behind me, and I need to ask him something."

"Who's Merle Brooks?"

"A postman. He said he saw Rylee's van at Oscar's place last week, but I don't know how, not when his route has him several miles from there at this time of day."

"Maybe he switches it up," Savannah suggested glibly. "I'll see you in a few."

The call ended and Ashley unbuckled her seat belt. "You stay in the back seat," she said to Max as she opened her door, leaving the motor running and the air conditioner on so Max would stay cool. She stepped out into the summer heat and closed the door behind her.

Merle parked behind her and stepped out of his vehicle. "Car trouble?" A broad smile creased his face as they neared each other.

"No, I was on a phone call and then saw you behind me. I wanted to ask you something."

Merle held up a glass soda bottle. "Can I get you one? I keep extras in a cooler."

"No thanks. I've got water in the console."

Merle bent to peer through the back window. "See you've got Max in there too. He sure is a fine dog."

"One of the best."

"Whatever happened to Oscar's dog? The boxer."

"A friend of mine is taking care of him this morning." Cliffy had gone with Josiah and his real estate agent, Luke Owens, to meet the owner of the property he was interested in. Luke had confirmed that the owner might be willing to sell if the price was right.

Perhaps that had something to do with why Savannah had returned to town so quickly. Ashley's imagination threatened to take off on a matrimonial rabbit trail, but she reined it in. There would be plenty of time for that later.

Merle took a long drink from the bottle. "What did you want to ask me?"

"I know this may sound strange." Ashley gave him a sheepish grin. "I saw you out this way last Thursday and again today, so I was wondering if this is your usual route."

"You're right. That is a strange question."

"So is it? Your usual route, I mean."

His eyes narrowed slightly as he studied her face, as if searching for the answer to a question he hadn't asked. Though his scrutiny made her uncomfortable, she didn't flinch or break the silence.

"Yeah," Merle finally said. "Customers expect their mail to arrive at about the same time every day. The morning folks in the morning. The afternoon folks in the afternoon. Why do you ask?"

"I guess I misunderstood what you told Chief Maloney about being near the Moore place at about this time last Tuesday. That's miles from here."

"You mean the day poor old Oscar was murdered." Merle bowed his head as if he still couldn't believe his friend was dead. "That was a sad day. A horrible day. I guess a lot of things could have gotten mixed up."

"The van you described was there that morning," Ashley said. "But I don't understand how you could have seen it."

He leaned against the front bumper of the mail truck and drained the rest of the soda from the bottle. "Seems you've figured out my secret," he said sadly. "I sure wish you'd kept your questions to yourself."

A tingle of fear raced up Ashley's spine. Since she'd stopped at the stop sign, not a single car had passed by. She could barely make out the nearest house through the surrounding trees. She folded her arms across her body, suddenly cold despite the heat of the day.

"I don't know your secret," she said. "I only wanted to know why you lied."

"It wasn't a lie. I saw the van."

"Rylee didn't kill Oscar."

"I know she didn't." He stared at Ashley, and she read the confession in his eyes.

Fear rooted Ashley to the ground, but she refused to panic. All she had to do was to keep him talking. Savannah would be passing that way soon. Maybe someone else would come by even sooner. *Just keep him talking.* "I thought you and Oscar were friends. What happened, Merle?"

"Oscar and me, we had an argument. Things got out of hand." His lower lip trembled. "I shouldn't have done it, but that Oscar—he had no right to say the things he did. To turn on me the way he did. Especially after all I'd done for him." His voice rose, and he pressed his thumb against his chest. "I knew who he was, but I never told anybody. He even dedicated one of his novels to me. 'To M.B.,' it says. 'A true and loyal friend.'" Merle snorted.

Ashley stood silent, afraid to move, afraid to speak.

Merle gulped in air, then shouted, "Oscar Moore was a fraud, and Ansel Dodger was a hack. And I told no one."

The shouting led Max to bark. Ashley tried to shush him, but for one of the rare times in his life, he didn't listen. Obviously disturbed by what was happening outside the vehicle, he repeatedly barked and tried to scramble over the back seat into the hatch.

Ashley started around the vehicle to calm him when the sharp crack of breaking glass added to Max's mayhem. She jerked back to look at Merle. He held the neck of the soda bottle in his hand. Glass shards littered the road between the two vehicles.

Merle waved the jagged edge of the bottle at Ashley. "You can't leave," he said. "Not now."

"I have to take care of Max." She tried to keep her voice soft and calm. "He needs me."

"Don't you dare let that dog out." Merle's wild-eyed expression was almost more frightening than the broken bottle he brandished as a weapon. All pretense of friendliness was gone.

Ashley scoured her mind for options. She could easily outrun the pudgy postman, except that would mean abandoning Max. That she couldn't do. Instead, she needed to talk him into letting her go. "You need to put that bottle down, Merle. Before someone gets hurt."

"I'm sorry to do this to you, Ashley." He shook his head as if with regret. "You're a nice gal, and I know a lot of people around here like you. But I can't let you go around telling people about me."

"I won't tell anyone."

"And I won't take that chance."

Ashley's gaze darted toward the other road, which Savannah would take to get to the alpaca farm. How much longer before she passed them? And what would happen when she did?

It'd be two against one, and Merle's weapon was improvised. The broken glass bottle could be deadly, but he couldn't take on both of them at the same time. However, while one called for help, the other might be seriously injured. No, she couldn't wish for Savannah to come sooner. Not when it might mean danger for her friend.

Merle closed the distance between them, gripped her arm with one hand, and pressed the broken end of the bottle against her ribs with the other. "Come with me."

He marched her behind the mail truck, then commanded her to lie down on the ground and close her eyes. She did as ordered, trying to ignore the pebbles and twigs digging into her skin. Her bigger problem was how to get out of the mess. She heard him rummaging around in the truck, then he pressed the bottle against her ribs again.

"I got a roll of duct tape here," he said. "Hands behind your back."

After he'd secured her hands and put another strip over her mouth, he pushed her into the rear of his truck. Her head smacked against the frame so hard she almost passed out. Once she was inside the truck, Merle covered her with an old blanket that smelled like a bad combination of fast food, sweaty gym clothes, and cigarette smoke. Ashley focused on breathing and not crying as Merle weighed down the blanket with packages. The heavy boxes squeezed her chest and made it impossible to move her legs.

At least Savannah would be driving by soon. She'd find Max alone in the Subaru. Nothing else mattered.

Savannah would rescue Max. It was the best Ashley could hope for.

21

The smelly blanket made Ashley's stomach churn. She twisted her head first one way, then the other until she found a small space where the blanket didn't threaten to smother her. The pounding in her head was in sync with the pounding in her heart. Her shoulders throbbed and her wrists felt assaulted by pins and needles. Though she wasn't claustrophobic, the awful blanket and the heavy weight of the packages against her body made her want to scream.

The mail truck had taken a right at the intersection, the opposite direction of town, and now it stopped. *Unbelievable!* While Merle held her hostage, he was still delivering the mail. That fact made her angry, but more than that, she was afraid.

Though he hadn't said the words, Merle had practically confessed to murdering Oscar. After killing one person, why would he hesitate to kill another? Somehow Ashley had to find a way out of this predicament, or at least keep Merle talking until help arrived.

When Savannah found Ashley's abandoned Subaru with her cell phone on the console and Max in the back, she'd call 911 and she'd call Cole. Both the Aspen Falls police department and the Eagle-Holy Cross Rangers would search for her. Savannah knew that Ashley had planned to talk to Merle. Everyone would be on the lookout for him too. If he kept delivering the mail as if nothing was wrong, then Ashley had time on her side.

The mail truck made two more stops, then navigated off the main road. Merle slowed to a crawl as the vehicle bumped along the unpaved road. He seemed to be trying to avoid potholes or ruts, though not with great success. Ashley tried to envision where Merle had turned. She'd driven these roads countless times for farm calls, but couldn't recall a side road in their current location.

A driveway.

That long, long driveway—she'd often passed it and wondered who lived at the other end. Was it Merle's home?

The mail truck stopped, and the driver's door slammed closed. The heavy packages were pushed off her body and the blanket yanked from her face. She blinked against a ray of sunlight piercing the side window.

"Come out of there." Merle yanked her out of the truck and gripped her arm until she caught her balance.

The two-story house, made of wood and stone, stood vacant and forlorn. The peeling paint, broken windows, and sagging porch indicated years of neglect. A rusted tricycle lay on its side in a weed-filled flower bed.

Ashley wanted to ask Merle who had lived here and what had happened to the family, but the duct tape covering her mouth made it impossible to talk. At least she could breathe easier without the blanket covering her face.

Merle retrieved the roll of duct tape, then pulled Ashley up the porch steps and through the front door. The foyer opened to a hallway with a long staircase leading to the second floor. Rooms opened up on both sides of the hall. He led her to one of the central rooms that had likely been a parlor or a dining room at one time. An old-fashioned fireplace with built-in cabinets on either side took up one wall. A trio of windows were joined together by a broad window seat.

"You'll stay here," Merle said, shoving her so that she fell to the floor. "I've got to finish my route and think about what to do with you." He held up the tape. "This is so you don't get any crazy ideas about leaving."

He removed her shoes and wound the duct tape tightly around her ankles. "I want you to know something about me killing Oscar. That was an accident. I've known about him being Ansel Dodger for years, and I was a big fan of his books. We'd get together sometimes, and I'd tell him about my ideas for a story of my own. I was going to call it *Tryst of Souls*."

Ashley's eyes widened. That was the name of the book she'd found on Oscar's back porch. The latest release from his literary alter ego.

"I see you've heard of it." Merle shook his head in disgust. "He took my title, my characters, my mythological setting. He took everything I spent years creating and made them his own. When I confronted him, he laughed. He said it was too good of a story to let a nobody like me write it. Can you believe that?"

I'm sorry. Even in this ridiculous circumstance, Ashley meant it. Ogden Sadler stole a dog. Oscar Moore stole six dogs. And Ansel Dodger stole a story. No matter his name, the murder victim had been a manipulative thief.

Merle knelt beside Ashley and placed his fingers on the edge of the tape covering her mouth. For a brief, hopeful moment, she thought he'd remove it. Instead, he gently pressed the edge down again.

"I know you have plenty to say to me." His voice was strangely kind, even gentle. "But it's too late for talk."

Without another word, he stood and walked out of the room, taking her shoes with him. Ashley rolled on her back and thumped her feet against the floor, but he didn't turn back. A few moments later, the mail truck roared to life, and Merle drove away.

If he thought she was going to wait around for him to come back, he could think again.

Ashley tried to reach the tape binding her ankles with her fingers, but that didn't work. Okay then, she'd simply hop to the road, no matter how long it took.

With a fair amount of effort, she rolled to the trio of windows. Bracing against the window seat and with a series of movements that tested her flexibility and strength, she managed to sit up and eventually stand. She hopped along the hall to the front door—only to find it closed and locked.

Now what?

When God closes a door, He opens a window.

Such a familiar saying, and the exact one Ashley needed at this moment. If she couldn't get out the door, she'd figure out a way to climb through a window. She maneuvered into one of the front rooms and smiled beneath the tape.

Shards of broken glass were scattered on the floor in front of the window. Other pieces were still embedded in the frame—pieces sharp enough to cut through tape.

Ashley hopped toward the window, doing her best to avoid the glass on the floor. When she reached the frame, she positioned her back toward it and twisted her neck to see over her shoulder. On her first and second attempts to get the glass in the narrow space between her bound hands, the sharp edge cut her skin, and she jerked away on reflex. Tears sprang to her eyes at the pain, but she couldn't give up. Merle might change his mind and come back for her at any moment.

She tried a third time and the tape stuck to the glass. With a careful sawing motion, she moved her hands against the glass until the edge of tape tore enough to give her more room to maneuver. Eventually she'd cut through enough of the tape that she was able to tear apart the rest.

She closed her eyes and breathed a prayer of thanks, then tugged at the tape covering her mouth. She loosened the top of the tape a small section at a time, enduring the pain while lacking the courage to rip it off with one fast yank. When her mouth was uncovered, she left the rest of the tape dangling on her chin like an unkempt goatee.

The base of her thumbs and her wrists were smeared with blood. She took off her socks and used one to clean herself up as well as she could without water. She used the other to protect her hand as she sliced through the tape around her feet with a broken shard.

Finally, she was free.

Without waiting a moment longer, she wrapped a sock around each hand, unlocked the front door, and headed down the long drive. Gravel poked at the soles of her bare feet, but she tried not to let the discomfort slow her down too much.

Instead, she focused on getting back to Max. On finding Savannah. On losing herself in Cole's embrace.

She felt sorry for Merle, she truly did. Oscar had stolen more than a story from the postman. He'd taken a treasured dream. But Merle's disappointment didn't give him the right to take Oscar's life, nor to steal Ashley's freedom to protect his own skin.

As she neared the road, she slowed her pace. If Merle returned, she wanted to see the mail truck before he spotted her. But no traffic interrupted the peaceful quiet of the rural Colorado area.

When she reached the road, Ashley headed toward where they'd left the Subaru, gingerly walking along the grassy shoulder to avoid burning her feet on the hot pavement. She hadn't gone far when she heard the low hum of a vehicle approaching her from behind. Since there was nowhere to hide, she moved farther into the ditch beside the road and prayed that the driver was someone on the way to Aspen Falls and not Merle. Though if she kept her distance from Merle, he couldn't harm her. It wouldn't be easy to outrun him when she was barefoot, but she'd do it.

She also prayed she wouldn't step on a snake.

As the vehicle came closer, Ashley's hope for rescue grew. The engine didn't sound at all like the mail truck. Confident Merle wasn't coming back for her, she returned to the road and waved her arms to flag down the driver.

A shiny, silver sedan braked to a stop and the driver emerged from the car.

"Savannah!" Ashley collapsed to the ground in relief. The aches and pains she'd ignored during the long, slow walk from the house now screamed for attention. The area around her mouth felt tender and she still wore the duct tape goatee. Her hands, wrapped in the bloody socks, throbbed, her shoulder muscles still ached, and her feet were raw.

Savannah rounded the sedan and knelt beside her. "What happened to you?" She brushed loose strands of hair from Ashley's face, her eyes wide with concern.

"I'm so glad to see you." She gulped air, finally able to breathe again now that the danger was over. "I thought you'd be on the other side of town by now." Her voice failed her and she took another deep breath.

"I got delayed by a herd of cattle who decided to take a stroll on the highway. I tried to call you—" Savannah's voice caught. "Ashley, what's going on?"

"My phone's in my Subaru. With Max." She tried to stand but her legs wouldn't support her. "We have to get to Max."

"We'll get him," Savannah reassured her. "Let me help you to the car."

Once they were in the sedan, Ashley practically melted into the cool leather seats. Her eyes barely open, she directed Savannah to where she'd left the Subaru and told her all about Merle.

Savannah parked beside the Subaru. Ashley's passenger door was parallel to her SUV's driver door, but Max was nowhere to be seen. Her heart in her throat, Ashley tried to unlatch her seat belt, but in her haste, it jammed.

Savannah put her hand on Ashley's arm. "You're not getting out of this car."

"He's gone." Ashley's voice cracked and tears burned the back of her eyes.

Savannah handed Ashley her phone. "Stay put and call 911." She popped out of the sedan and sprinted to the Subaru as Ashley rolled down her window.

"The driver's door is locked." Savannah shaded her eyes to peer into the window, then faced Ashley, the worry in her eyes replaced with delight. "He's not here. Someone must have found him."

Ashley wasn't sure whether to be relieved or even more worried.

Savannah must have seen her uncertainty. "I'm sure he's safe. A Good Samaritan probably came by, saw him, and took him to town."

"What if Merle came back for him?"

"Why would he do that?"

"So I'd do what he wanted when he came back for me."

Savannah touched Ashley's shoulder. "We'll find Max," she said quietly. "I promise we will."

Ashley shook her head, avoiding Savannah's gaze as she tried to get her chaotic emotions under control.

"Hold on a second." Savannah moved to the front of the Subaru and reached across the windshield. She waved a folded piece of paper. "Look what I found under the windshield wiper."

"What does it say?"

Savannah opened the note. "It's from Rob Tavish. 'Found Max alone and couldn't find you so I'm taking him to town. Grabbed your purse and keys, but left your phone so you can let us know where you are if you come back. Search party on the way. Call me.' See, Ashley? Max is fine."

Waves of relief flowed over Ashley as tears dampened her cheeks. She tried to wipe them away with her sock-wrapped hand.

"But you're not," Savannah continued. "I'm taking you to the medical center now." She rounded the sedan and climbed in. "Did you call 911?"

"I was too worried about Max."

"I understand that kind of worry. Believe me, I do." Savannah latched her seat belt. "But now it's time to take care of you. And to let everyone know you're okay. Rob probably called Cole to see if he knew where you were. Imagine how worried he must be."

"I should call him."

"Yeah, you should."

Still, Ashley hesitated, though she couldn't say why. He needed to know that she was fine. Or that she would be fine. But the nightmare with Merle wasn't over yet. It wouldn't be until he was behind bars. "We need to find Merle," Ashley said firmly.

Savannah gaped at Ashley in the midst of maneuvering a three-point turn. "Are you crazy? Did you hit your head or something?"

"Not to confront him. Just to keep an eye on him so he can't go on the run."

"I don't know about that." Savannah stopped at the intersection and studied both directions as if trying to decide which way to go. Left toward town? Or right to follow Merle's route?

"A search party is already on its way," Ashley insisted. "That means the police department, which means the search party can easily become the 'take down Merle' party."

Savannah chuckled at the description. "You win." She flipped her blinker to indicate a right turn. "But you're not to get out of this car under any circumstances. I mean it."

"I won't." Ashley awkwardly tried to pick up Savannah's phone. But the socks and the blood on her hands made it impossible.

Savannah noticed Ashley's struggle and quickly connected a call to Chief Maloney through the sedan's speaker system.

When the chief answered, Ashley wasted no time blurting out, "Merle Brooks killed Oscar Moore."

"Ashley?" the chief asked. "Where are you?"

"With Savannah. We're driving Merle's postal route."

"Everyone's looking for you," Maloney said. "I'm only about a mile away from where Rob said he found your Subaru."

"Coming from town?" Ashley asked, and the chief confirmed her guess. "Keep going straight. You're not that far behind us."

"You're sure Merle Brooks is the murderer?" Chief Maloney sounded skeptical. "What possible motive could he have?"

"Oscar stole his dream." Ashley grimaced, her head suddenly feeling as if it were about to explode. With all her other injuries causing so much grief, she'd almost forgotten striking her head against the mail truck, but her awareness of it had grown since Savannah had asked about it. She closed her eyes against a light that suddenly seemed too bright.

"Ashley?" Savannah's voice echoed at an unnaturally loud volume in her ears.

She tried to swipe the sound away and smiled when Savannah's words faded into nothingness.

When Ashley opened her eyes, she was on a gurney by the side of the road with Cole on one side and Savannah on the other.

"Hello, sleepyhead." Tenderness mingled with concern in Cole's green eyes. "I heard you've had quite a morning."

Ashley reached up to stroke his shaven chin. Bandages had replaced the bloody socks on her hands. "I miss your beard."

He smiled. "I'll grow it back when the weather changes."

"How did you get here?" Ashley asked.

"I was part of the convoy sent out to find you," he answered.

"Fortunately, the ambulance was too. I need you to promise never to scare me like this again. Please, Ash."

"I don't think she can make that promise." Savannah grinned down at her. "Not from the stories I've heard."

"Did you catch Merle?" Ashley asked.

"He's in handcuffs and on his way to a holding cell right next to Valerie Nelson." Savannah gave an unladylike snort. "Though I suppose they won't be able to hold her much longer. She still insists she had nothing to do with the dog theft."

"The crime lab will find the evidence," Cole reassured her. "Just give them time."

The EMTs returned to slide the gurney into the ambulance.

Cole pressed his lips against Ashley's, a soft and gentle kiss. "See you at the medical center."

Suddenly too tired to respond, Ashley closed her eyes and allowed sleep to overtake her once again. As she did, she smiled, secure in the knowledge that her nightmares wouldn't be back.

22

The picturesque sunrise heralded a perfect day in the mountains for the participants of the Eagle County Adventure Race. Vendor booths were set up at Silver Bend Park, a riverside recreation area on the outskirts of town and the final checkpoint of the day's events. Visitors could purchase baked goods supplied by Three Peaks Bakery or check out the latest sports gear from White River Outfitters and North Woods Sports Rental.

One section of the Silver Bend grounds was set apart for the competitors. The Talons Grip and Fighting Fit teams had claimed spots next to each other. Canopies decorated with red and blue bandannas respectively provided shade to the crew members while they waited for their team to approach the finish line. The other checkpoints along the race weren't as elaborate. There were no vendor booths, but each one had a medical tent. Most crew chiefs had erected small tents where the competitors could quickly change from hiking gear to biking gear to kayak gear.

The rules for the competition were simple. Starting times were staggered to avoid congestion. A minimum fifteen-minute break was required between each activity. The team that completed all three legs of the course in the shortest amount of time was declared the winner.

Though more than a week had passed since her encounter with Merle and Ashley felt fine, Dr. Quinn had dissuaded her from being an active crew team member due to her recent head trauma. Savannah took her place, which meant she helped Rob ensure clothing and gear were easily accessible to the team at each checkpoint, provided energy bars and plenty of water, and took care of any other details that popped up.

When Ashley and Rylee, who had been released from the medical center a couple days earlier, promised to spend most of the day in their chairs, they were named honorary crew members so they could cheer for Cole, Josiah, and Lorie. They also encouraged the other local team members—Corey Astin, Dina Ford, and Nate Emerson, the owner of White River Outfitters.

The starting point was located near the Eagle-Holy Cross Ranger Station in the White River National Forest. Teams were given GPS devices and coordinates to help them navigate their way through the forest to the first checkpoint, where they exchanged hiking boots and walking sticks for bicycles and helmets. The path was well-marked, but at times required carrying bikes over stream beds or rough terrain.

The next checkpoint was located near a primitive camping site on the Eagle River. From there, the competitors launched their kayaks for the final leg of the competition and headed toward Silver Bend.

Ashley and Rylee sat in camp chairs under the Talons Grip canopy while Savannah explored the vendor booths. Rob divided his time between the canopy and the administration tent where volunteers recorded the teams' starting and finishing times for each event. He carried a clipboard where he copied the times for each team.

The good news was that Talons Grip and Fighting Fit had come in first and second in the hiking leg. However, they'd slipped to fifth and fourth in the biking leg. A team from Vail was their strongest competition, placing third in hiking and first in biking. Since the total time for all three events mattered most, the three teams were in the running to win the competition. It all came down to how quickly they navigated the river.

Savannah returned to the canopy with frozen lemonade for each of them. Ashley smiled as Rylee accepted the drink. The young woman seemed in awe of Savannah, who was determined for them to be friends.

The district attorney had yet to file specific charges, so Rylee's future was still uncertain. The accident and murder accusations had been the wake-up call the young woman needed to turn her life around. She was living with Josiah, who'd rented the ten-acre property and was in the middle of purchase negotiations with the owner. Cliffy lived there too. As soon as Dr. Quinn gave her the go-ahead, Rylee would be waiting tables at Icebreakers Pub.

Ashley glanced at her watch. "How much longer do you think it'll be?"

"The first kayakers passed the midpoint about ten minutes ago," Savannah said. "They still have quite a way to go."

Wendy Heath, wearing her uniform, rapped on a pole. "Knock, knock. Okay if I come in?"

"Please do." Savannah pulled a vacant chair closer to the group. "It's good to see you again. Is Andie here?"

"She's with a couple of friends," Wendy replied as she took the seat. "I'm sure she'll stop by to see you."

"I hope so," Savannah said. "If we don't meet up today, then maybe we'll run into each other at church tomorrow."

"How long will you be in town?" Wendy asked.

"Not long this time around." Savannah's smile broadened and her eyes twinkled. "But come fall, you'll be seeing a lot more of me."

Ashley was already privy to Savannah's plans. She and Josiah hoped to plan a life together, but they wanted to spend plenty of time getting to know each other before taking the matrimonial leap. Since Josiah hadn't been in Aspen Falls very long, he'd been willing to move to Amarillo. However, Savannah hadn't been exaggerating when she said on her first trip to the small town that she'd fallen in love with it. She was excited for the change. Since she owned her own business, she could live wherever she wanted.

"I'm glad to hear it," Wendy said. "Anytime you need a pet sitter for Bridey, be sure to let us know."

"About that," Savannah began, eager to share more fun news. "Bridey's mama is due to have a litter in about four to five weeks. I'm a part owner, and this time I get pick of the litter. Now that all this mess is behind us, please let me choose a puppy for Andie as my gift for how well she took care of Bridey."

"A puppy like that must cost a fortune," Wendy said. "That's not fair to you."

"It's the least I can do for the way you and your family stepped up in such an awful situation. I don't know what I would have done if you hadn't given Bridey a safe place to land," Savannah answered firmly. "Besides, Bridey and I are ready to retire from the dog show world."

"Andie would never forgive me if I said no." Wendy reached for Savannah's hand. "Thank you."

When Savannah had said "this mess is behind us," Rylee's cheeks had flushed, and she'd hung her head. Ashley sensed that guilt would be with her for a long time despite Savannah's wholehearted forgiveness.

"It's good to see you out and about, Ms. Goodwin," Wendy said softly. "You look much better than the last time I saw you."

"Oh, I'm sorry," Ashley said. "I should have introduced you. Rylee, this is Officer Wendy Heath. She was one of the first responders at the accident site."

"You were pretty banged up then," Wendy said. "Our family has been praying for you every day since."

"You have?" Rylee asked.

"Absolutely." Wendy gave her a gracious smile. "I hear you're going to be staying here in Aspen Falls too. Welcome to your new home."

"Thank you." Rylee wore a cautious expression, as if she couldn't believe anyone would truly welcome her, but Ashley hoped in time that she'd realize Wendy meant what she'd said. She could have a new start here, as long as she truly wanted one.

They chatted with Wendy for a while longer, and she brought them up-to-date on the Valerie Nelson and Merle Brooks investigations. Both individuals were now incarcerated elsewhere.

Once the crime lab tracked Valerie's posts on the message board, she confessed that she'd been in love with the man she knew as C.G., even though they'd never met. Through messages and texts, he made her believe he loved her too. The cause had to come first, though.

Then Rylee had shown up and become C.G.'s new favorite. Valerie had been heartbroken when Rylee was given the privilege of taking the stolen dogs to C.G.'s home, where she'd get to meet him in person. So Valerie had hatched her own plan. She was supposed to drive Rylee's car, an old beater, from the rest stop and ditch it somewhere after dumping all the dogs' personal belongings in another location that would muddy the investigation if they were discovered. Instead, she'd put a GPS tracker on her own van and had her motorcycle parked at the rest area.

Using the tracker, she followed Rylee to Oscar Moore's home. Since she didn't want to create a scene, she left for about ten minutes, then came back again in hopes that Rylee would be gone and she could spend time with C.G. by herself. When she discovered C.G.'s body, she assumed Rylee had killed him. In a jealous rage, she'd tracked the van and run it off the road.

Ashley already knew most of Merle's story, but Wendy provided a new detail. Merle, not Katee Havenstar, had posted Oscar's manuscript pages. According to Merle, Oscar had ordered him to leave and never come back, but Merle had wanted compensation for Oscar's plagiarizing of his story. He'd threatened to take Oscar to court. Oscar attacked him, and Merle had killed him in self-defense.

That part of the narrative was questionable since Oscar had been stabbed in the back, but Merle insisted that was what had happened. He'd also mentioned that Cliffy hadn't been inside the house when he and Oscar had argued, but the general assumption was that Cliffy had come in from the yard just as Merle was leaving to find his owner dead, then run off to chase Merle. It was only by chance that Cliffy had ended up in the same vicinity as the van crash. Fortunately, the boxer had forgotten his traumatic experience and would live out his years happily with Josiah and Savannah. The rest of Merle's life wouldn't be so happy—with the additional charges of kidnapping Ashley and threatening her life, Merle Brooks would no doubt spend the rest of his days in prison.

Other friends stopped by the canopied tent, eager to check on Ashley and meet Rylee and Savannah. Before long, Rob raced in with the news that the kayakers were in the final stretch of the river. They all hurried to the stands that had been set up for the onlookers.

Seven kayakers were grouped together with two more trailing by less than fifty yards. "Our teams and the Vail team are all neck and neck," Rob said. "From this distance, I can't be sure who the two are in the back, though."

"Josiah's in first." Rylee's voice held more excitement than Ashley had ever heard from her. "I know that's him."

"I think you're right." Savannah wrapped an arm around Rylee. "He's going to win. And look, Ashley. There's Cole right behind him."

"I see him." Despite the noise around her, she focused solely on him until all other sounds and all the other racers faded away. He glanced her way, and as impossible as it seemed considering the crowd around her, she knew that the impromptu grin that crinkled his eyes was meant for her. He might be about to win a race, but more importantly, he'd won her heart.

YOUR FEEDBACK MEANS A LOT TO US!

Up to this point, we've been doing all the writing. Now it's *your* turn!

Tell us what you think about this book, the characters, the bad guy, or anything else you'd like to share with us about this series. We can't wait to hear from *you*!

Log on to give us your feedback at:

https://www.surveymonkey.com/r/MysteriesAspen

Annie's® FICTION

Learn more about Annie's fiction books at

AnniesFiction.com

We've designed the website especially for you!

Access your e-books and audiobooks* • Manage your account

Choose from these great series:

Amish Inn Mysteries
Annie's Attic Mysteries
Annie's Museum of Mysteries
Annie's Mystery Quilt Stitch Along
Annie's Mysteries Unraveled
Annie's Quilted Mysteries
Annie's Secrets of the Quilt
Annie's Sweet Intrigue
Antique Shop Mysteries
Chocolate Shoppe Mysteries
Creative Woman Mysteries
Hearts of Amish Country
Inn at Magnolia Harbor
Love in Lancaster County
Mistletoe Mysteries
Mysteries of Aspen Falls
Rose Cottage Book Club
Secrets of the Castleton Manor Library
Scottish Bakehouse Mysteries
Victorian Mansion Flower Shop Mysteries

THREE FORMATS FOR YOUR CONVENIENCE

HARDCOVER

E-BOOK

AUDIOBOOK*

*available in select series only

What are you waiting for? Annie's® FICTION